I'LL WAIT F...

Maggie is engaged to Joel, and when he asks her to go to Russia with him she thinks it is going to be a wonderful holiday for two. But then she discovers that Joel's ex-girlfriend, Bebe, and his brother, Drew, are going too! The uneasy foursome sets off, but Drew's behaviour puzzles Maggie. Why the sudden decision to go to Russia, and without his beautiful wife, Irina? And why does she see him deep in conversation with a Russian in a Moscow street?

Books by Maureen Stephenson
in the Linford Romance Library:

AUTUMN OF DECEPTION
ROSES HAVE THORNS
THE LOVE DANCE

MAUREEN STEPHENSON

◆

I'LL WAIT FOREVER

Complete and Unabridged

LINFORD
Leicester

First published in Great Britain in 1987

First Linford Edition
published 1996

British Library CIP Data

Stephenson, Maureen
   I'll wait forever.—Large print ed.—
Linford romance library
   1. English fiction—20th century
   2. Large type books
   I. Title
823.9'14 [F]

ISBN 0–7089–7969–6

Published by
F. A. Thorpe (Publishing) Ltd.
Anstey, Leicestershire

Set by Words & Graphics Ltd.
Anstey, Leicestershire
Printed and bound in Great Britain by
T. J. Press (Padstow) Ltd., Padstow, Cornwall

This book is printed on acid-free paper

1

IT started to rain as Maggie turned her car onto the narrow road that wound its way across Mirbeck Moor, a desolate bleak area at this time of the year with just her father's sheep grazing amongst dead bracken and heather. In the distance the fells of the Lake District lay enveloped in a thick shroud of mist.

The news she had received that afternoon that the Lazonby Repertory Theatre was closing seemed to have deadened her senses. Even though she had known its future was shaky Maggie, the eternal optimist, had always felt something would happen, but nothing had, except for the theatre director to announce its closure.

Her thoughts turned to her mother, a pretty fair-haired woman who had had ambitions to become an actress, and

1

when Maggie had shown an interest in the theatre she had been delighted and encouraged it. It had been tragic when she had died, and a few years later when Maggie had entered drama school she had been happy knowing she was fulfilling her mother's dearest wish.

Then life had taken a sudden unexpected twist and the summer she had graduated her father had inherited his brother's Cumbrian farm and made the surprising decision to terminate his job as estate manager for the Brooksbys and run the farm himself.

"I know people will think I'm mad giving up a good job at Kingsley Magna," he had told Maggie. "But that farm's been in the Kerr family two centuries and I've got to keep up the family tradition and run it."

Maggie was worried about her father's health. Hill farming was tough for the young. She was undecided what to do. Then she heard of the vacancy at Lazonby, some fifteen miles from

2

Mirbeck and got the job. Now it seemed her luck had run out.

The road now dipped into a small valley where on the far slope the farmhouse perched between rocky boulders; its stone walls whitewashed, its roof of weathered green tiles. Always a welcoming landmark and particularly so tonight as daylight faded and a mist started to mushroom in the bottom of the valley.

Slowing her car down she crossed the old wooden bridge that spanned the roaring mountain - stream, then cautiously proceeded up the muddied track on the other side of the torrent, past a small walled garden and entered the farmyard. Immediately a black-and-white sheep dog sprang to meet her, and as she stepped out of the car she jumped at her excitedly, her muddy paws marking her pale skirt.

"Down Polly. You've ruined my new skirt," she replied crossly. Then someone whistled and the dog bounded off. Maggie looked up to see her father standing at the door, a tall, grey-haired man with a weather-beaten complexion.

"Sorry I'm late, Dad," she called. "But the meeting went on longer than I thought."

She followed him into a cosy comfortable room, where a good fire blazed and the polished horse brass gleamed overhead on the dark oak beams.

She would have to tell him, she thought, as she stood a moment warming herself in front of the fire. And how she hated being the bearer of bad news, particularly when all was not well on the farm. Last spring her father had had a high percentage of pregnancy toxaemia in the ewes. The vet had said it was due to the higher than average rainfall the previous winter and poor quality hay, and that was due to the higher than usual rainfall the previous summer. It's a hard life farming in the Lake District, she thought ruefully, as she walked across to join her father in the kitchen.

Mr Kerr was filling the kettle at the sink and the room was filled with the delicious aroma of roast lamb.

"Why did you have to go to a meeting Sunday afternoon?" he asked looking over his shoulder.

"The only time the director could get everyone together. I'm afraid I've got bad news. The theatre closes next Saturday night — it's going to be turned into a bingo hall."

"But why?" he asked looking perplexed. "I saw one of your plays last summer and I thought it damn good, and you were particularly good, Maggie, as the young wife who . . . "

"It's nothing to do with the quality of the plays," Maggie tried to explain. "It's financial problems."

"I'm sorry to hear it. What are you going to do now?"

"I've got to get another job, but it's going to be difficult," she replied delving into the sack and starting to peel the potatoes.

"Chips all right, Dad? They're quicker."

That was one thing she didn't have to worry about. Whatever she ate her figure remained as trim as ever. Perfect metabolism she had told her envying friends at Lazonby. What she wished she had was capital to start her own theatrical company but that was beyond the realms of possibility so she had better stop thinking about it.

It was when they sat down to eat that Mr Kerr remembered the phone call.

"Joel phoned this afternoon," he said helping himself to the mint sauce. "Said he'd phone back later."

Maggie brightened visibly at this, nothing like a fiancé to lean on in times of trouble she thought with a smile. I am lucky. Whatever happens I have Joel. Dear sweet, kind Joel.

What extraordinary luck it had been meeting him at the Royal Show last summer. He had been delighted to see her again, in fact overwhelmingly so. It had surprised her for all the years she had lived on the Kingsley Magna estate his attitude towards her had been one of restraint, rather like a disinterested brother. He had invited her out to dinner that night and in the intervening months visited Mirbeck Farm several times, and on the last visit dining by candlelight at Yewbarrow Grange over a bottle of Château Neuf had proposed.

Maggie's reaction had been one of sheer astonishment. Never in her wildest dreams had she thought of Joel as a lover, more a friend and a good one. His kisses were clumsy and schoolboyish, but she felt relaxed in his company. Joel was a link with her childhood, the difficult years of growing up. He had been part of her life for so many years it seemed the right thing to do. She had accepted. Another important factor she had reached the grand old age of twenty-five.

As she put the dirty dishes onto a tray the phone rang in the hall. Her father went to answer it.

"Maggie? Yes, she's here Joel. Just hang on a moment while I tell her. Maggie," he called. "It's Joel."

Maggie put down the tray and hurried into the hall picking up the receiver.

"Hello, Joel. Just the person I want to speak to. Something awful's happened. The job at Lazonby's finished. It was expected but it's still a shock. Anyway it was a wonderful experience and a first-rate company. Know anyone who wants a blue-eyed redhead, five foot six inches with four years rep. experience. You do! You're very sweet Joel." Then her expression changed to one of surprise. "Did you say Russia? Would I like to join a party from your college. I'm not sure what to do. I'm supposed to be going to London to look for a job. No I'm not afraid of the K.G.B." she laughed. "I'll phone you back as soon as I can."

Maggie put the phone down and returned to the dining-room.

"Joel wants me to go to Russia with

him," she told her father.

Mr Kerr completed the task of putting coal on the fire and straightened up.

"What on earth does he want to go there for?"

"He's taking a degree in Russian Studies and wants to have a look at Moscow and Leningrad universities to see which one he likes best. He has to spend a year in the U.S.S.R. as part of the course."

Mr Kerr was not impressed. "I thought he had a degree in English."

"He has that as well. But he thought Russian would open up more career opportunities."

"That young man's a permanent student," remarked Mr Kerr dryly. "And life's one long holiday. What are you going to do?"

"I said I'd let him know."

The following week there was such an air of despondency backstage at the Lazonby Theatre, plus the fact that her agent had nothing to offer her, that on the Wednesday night Maggie phoned Joel to say she would go with him. It turned out to be a good decision because during the intervening weeks before departure Maggie attended two auditions was turned down at both, and each rejection ate away at her self-confidence so that when the first week in November arrived she was glad to pack her bag and go.

It had been arranged she should meet Joel at Kingsley Magna Hall, staying overnight and leaving for Gatwick first thing the following morning in Joel's car.

Waving goodbye to her father, Maggie set off in her little car on the first stage of her journey, and all the way down the motorway she was in high spirits. It was when she stopped for a meal break she hoped his brother Drew would not be at Kingsley Magna when she arrived. There was a good chance he would not be there. Joel had often told her he was frequently away on business trips for he was now making a name

10

for himself in the electronics field.

Why had there always been conflict between Drew and herself? Being five years her senior had not helped. Being tough and superior hadn't either.

With sinking spirits she recalled her sixteenth birthday. Why she thought of it at that precise moment she couldn't really say, but the pain was as sharp as ever.

She had brought the dress with her birthday money. Ridiculous now when she thought of it, slinky tight black satin with a see-through top and plunging neckline. She decided to wear it at the Brooksbys' Christmas dance the following week and the sole object was to impress Drew.

She hero-worshipped him with his fast sports cars, the neck-breaking climbing expeditions he went on, which in her eyes gave him extraordinary charisma, but more important when she was ten he had fished her out of the moat. If he hadn't been passing by she would certainly have drowned.

11

This incident only served to increase the hero-worshipping. Unfortunately she had reached the sophisticated age of sixteen and he still treated her as though she were a child. Well she'd show him she was a real woman.

So on the night of the dance she had got into this black creation, piled her hair up, applied green eye make-up, blusher, and lipstick. She had felt pleased with the result as she stood in front of the mirror. Added at least ten years to her age she thought. Then walking across to the hall had mingled with the guests in the tapestry room.

Suddenly she had felt Drew's eyes upon her but to her surprise they were full of derision. He had asked her to dance and as they had glided about the floor his lips were twitching with laughter.

"What are you dressed up for like that?" he had asked at length when the music stopped.

"I don't know what you are talking about," she had replied determined to

12

ignore the banter that was obviously coming.

"I think you do."

They stood there glaring at each other on the dance floor.

"Why are you being rude to me?"

"Because you look like a tart in that get-up. Go home and take it off and never let me see you in it again."

The music started for the next dance and couples moved onto the floor. Maggie's hand went up and she hit Drew across the face, before running across the dance floor, then up the stairs that led to the long gallery. She heard a footstep behind her, then Drew placed his hand on her arm.

"I was a bit brutal but I felt it was the only way."

She turned and faced him. "The only way?"

"Yes. You're still a child; you need guidance."

"I am not a child," she replied defiantly. "And I don't need any guidance from anyone."

"Prove to me you're not a child," he said suddenly taking her in his arms. Then his mouth had seared hers, pushing her lips apart his tongue had teased hers, whilst his hands groped to find her young nipples.

Trembling, shaken and pale she had pulled away feeling violated, used.

"How dare you."

"See you are still a child," he had repeated.

She had run down the long gallery, out of the hall, and back to their cottage, where she had run up to her room and wept angry tears thinking how much she hated Drew Brooksby. When she was tired of crying she had looked at herself in the mirror. He was right, she looked awful but why couldn't he have been a little kinder? She had taken the dress off and flung it to the back of the wardrobe. She had never worn it again.

Maggie got back into her car in a more sober mood. She had avoided Drew for a long time after that and when avoidance had been impossible she had been cold and hostile. How right her decision had been to marry Joel; so kind and amenable, their marriage was so obviously going to be a success.

When she left the motorway and the road ran between lush Warwickshire meadows and placidly moving rivers her good spirits returned. Whatever had happened in the past her overall memories of Kingsley Magna were happy ones. She was going home. The feeling was not surprising, the Brooksby estate had been her home for most of her life.

There was no gate to Kingsley Magna Hall, just an unmade drive leading off the road with the notice PRIVATE in large black letters marking the entrance. It had been like that as long as she could remember. She turned the car into the drive, the ancient oak trees meeting overhead so that on hot summer days the drive had been a cool retreat.

And when the long drive came to

an end and the trees ceased suddenly, to the right lay the house — Kingsley Magna Hall, rising from the moat like a vision from a fairy-tale. It never failed to thrill her — the sight of that medieval house built of grey stone with its tall red Tudor chimneys and the bridge over the moat leading to the heavily panelled nail-studded oak door. And above the door was the great mullioned and transomed window. As a small girl she used to imagine medieval ladies in their wimples and coifs sitting there working at their tapestry.

Maggie parked her car by the old stable block, noticing with a smile the clock in the tower still pointed at ten to twelve, then crossing the bridge she pulled the bell handle by the door. There was a distant familiar tinkling sound followed by a dog barking. A few moments later the door was opened by the housekeeper Mrs Meeson. Maggie recognized her round homely face immediately as she bent to pat the golden labrador.

"Hello, Mrs Meeson," said Maggie. But the elderly woman's face was a blank. Then suddenly recognition dawned.

"Maggie!" she exclaimed smiling. "I would never have known you. How you've changed."

She stood a moment surveying her taking in the smart tailored suit, the stylish haircut. "Come in. We can't stand talking here."

Maggie followed her through a stone archway into an inner courtyard filled with flower beds of late flowering chrysanthemums and clipped yew hedges, then into the house on the south side.

"How's your father keeping?" Mrs Meeson asked pausing in a small oak-panelled hall.

"He's very well thank you. And how are you?"

"Not so bad. My arthritis keeps playing me up but what can you expect surrounded by water. Still I'm not grumbling. Now I think it's Joel you'll be wanting," she added a big smile lighting up her face. "Congratulations. And fancy me not recognising you."

She showed Maggie into a large high room that had once been the great hall. On the far wall hung a tapestry. Maggie knew every detail of that eighteenth-century picnic scene with the men in their tricorne hats and the women in panniered gowns and shepherdess hats.

"Things haven't been the same since your father left," commented Mrs Meeson closing the door. "Then there was all that business of Mrs Brooksby going off to the States and Mr Brooksby taken ill. I like things to remain as they are. Still there's no point in grumbling." She indicated a large leather armchair before the great stone fireplace where a log fire blazed. Maggie sat down. "Joel tells me you're off to Russia," she continued. "If you've got any sense you won't go. You can't trust those Russians. Now you be careful," she warned.

"I will," Maggie laughed. "How's Mr Brooksby?"

"Very weak and there's no improvement in his speech. I doubt if he'll ever talk again. Like to see him?"

"I would."

"It's best if we go now before he has his afternoon nap."

Mrs Meeson and Maggie went up the stairs and along the corridor to Mr Brooksby's room where they found him seated in a wheelchair by the window watching a couple of blackbirds eating breadcrumbs on the window ledge outside. The sound of them entering the room made him turn. Maggie looked at his dry grey face, his emaciated body and remembered how he used to be. His thin hand grasped hers.

"Remember Maggie Kerr?" said Mrs Meeson looking at him kindly.

He smiled. He remembered.

"How are you?" Maggie asked politely.

"Maggie is off to Russia," Mrs Meeson told him.

His smile was switched off and he frowned.

"You don't think I should go?" asked Maggie puzzled at the change in him.

In reply he made an indistinguishable sound trying to speak, the colour rising in his face.

"We have to go now. I don't think we should tire him," advised Mrs Meeson giving Maggie a warning look.

"Good-bye Mr Brooksby," said Maggie. "Nice to see you again."

They left the room and walked back down the corridor to the tapestry room.

"Mr Brooksby thinks I shouldn't go," said Maggie thoughtfully.

"Oh don't worry your head about him," came the reply. "He's not living in your world." But Maggie had a strong suspicion he was, very much so. She shrugged off the mood as Mrs Meeson opened the door of the great, high room.

"I'll go and see if I can find Mr Joel."

She hurried off leaving Maggie alone.

In the corner the grandfather clock ticked away and on the walls hung the portraits of hedonistic Elizabethans in their lace ruffles and embroidered clothes, stern-faced Puritans in their black tunics and hats, and on the wall between the windows a grave-looking Victorian. He was an ancestor of Drew and Joel's, who having amassed a fortune as a tobacco importer had bought Kinglsey Magna in the first half of the last century.

Suddenly footsteps sounded in the corridor outside and Maggie turned, eager and expectant as the door opened and Joel came in, — tall and lanky, his fair curly hair brushed back and at the sight of Maggie a boyish grin broke out over his face.

To Maggie's surprise a young woman was with him, blonde, pretty in white trousers and loose purple satin blouse. She was very pretty but her mouth was set in a petulant expression which rather spoilt the effect.

Joel walked across to Maggie and

planted a kiss on her cheek.

"Lovely to see you, Maggie. Good journey? Mini behaved herself?"

"Perfectly."

Then following Maggie's enquiring eyes Joel turned to his companion.

"This is Bebe. She's an American from college — she's coming with us."

"Hi!" Bebe greeted her with a wave of her hand.

"Hi!" Maggie returned the greeting. Joel hadn't mentioned a word about an American girl coming.

"Guy and Jeff dropped out at the last minute," explained Joel. "Pity, you would have liked them. Cup of coffee?"

"Love it," smiled Maggie, watching Joel leave the room. So it was just going to be the three of them. She wasn't sure she liked it. She turned to Bebe who had slumped into an armchair, a miserable expression clouding her blue eyes.

"Sorry. Looks as though I'll be

playing gooseberry to you and Joel."

"Of course you won't," lied Maggie bravely. "I'm sure the three of us will get on famously."

"I'd better explain why Guy's not coming," she continued her eyes brimming with tears. "We had an awful row and split up."

"I'm sorry to hear that," commiserated Maggie.

"Guy said the most terrible things and it's all untrue. I've never been out with Jeff in my life let alone had an affair with him. I wanted to cancel this trip but Joel wouldn't hear of it."

"You're all on the Russian Studies course," asked Maggie sitting down opposite.

"Too true."

At that moment the door opened and Joel entered carrying a tray bearing three cups of coffee. He set the tray down and handed round the coffee.

"Thanks, Joel," said Bebe. "I was just telling Maggie I wanted to cancel the trip but you wouldn't hear of it."

"Of course I wouldn't," he replied fervently. "She must come, mustn't she Maggie. It will help her to forget."

"Of course it will," agreed Maggie.

Bebe took a sip at the coffee and a tear rolled down her cheek.

"I'll never forget your kindness, never."

They sat a few minutes drinking the coffee and discussing the forthcoming trip.

"We're going to have a great time," said Joel enthusiastically.

"What time do we leave in the morning," asked Maggie.

"Very early start I'm afraid. I think it a good idea if we put the luggage in the boot now."

"I'm having awful trouble with my suitcase, Joel," Bebe's voice whined. "I've crammed so much in I can't get it shut. Do you think you could give me a hand?"

She started walking towards the door. Joel bent over Maggie, an apologetic look on his face.

"Sorry about this Maggie," he whispered. "I hope you don't mind, but the poor kid's been absolutely distraught."

"Of course, Joel," Maggie assured him. "Don't give it another thought."

"I knew you'd think like that. Oh by the way, Drew's coming."

"Drew!" exclaimed Maggie, startled at this information. "You never said Drew was coming."

"Didn't I? Oh sorry about that. It was a last-minute decision — surprised me actually."

"What about Irina?"

"She must be away on tour and he's at a loose end. Drew's still the same — not forthcoming about himself. See you in a moment."

As he closed the door Maggie moved across to the window and looked down at the moat, the water smooth as silk; two swans glided past making a gentle ripple upon the surface of the water.

She remembered the time she had seen Irina dance in 'Swan Lake'. She was the most beautiful creature she had ever seen. No wonder Drew had fallen in love with her. It was all due to Julie Harris. Julie was an old school friend. She had been studying ballet for many years and had finally been accepted by the Royal Westminster Ballet Company.

She had phoned Maggie one day inviting her to the last night of the London season and the party that followed. Bring Drew and Joel she had added. So the three of them had gone, and at the end of the performance when the audience had departed, together with the other guests they had gone up onto the stage and sipped champagne with the company.

Julie had introduced them to Irina Doestraskaya and lost what faint interest Drew had had in her. She could see Irina now, with her black hair parted in the centre and plaited into a coronet on top of her head, her high cheek-bones, her large expressive eyes. Her every movement gracious perfection.

She had made Maggie feel like a clumsy cart-horse.

It was obvious from the start they were deeply attracted. Maggie had felt surprisingly resentful. She wasn't sure why because she did not like Drew. She didn't trust him. Soon after she and her father had moved north she had received an invitation to the wedding. She hadn't gone. She was playing in a matinée that afternoon and had no understudy. It was a good excuse.

"Hello, Maggie!"

Drew's sudden, rich resonant voice startled her from her daydreams. She turned quickly to see him standing in the doorway. Just as good-looking as ever, but older, more mature than she remembered. He walked across the room in that quick impatient way of his and grasped her hand. There were a few grey hairs at the temple, new lines about the jaw, but he was still the same, his mouth still had that hard firmness about it.

"Sorry I startled you, Maggie." Then

his face relaxed into a smile. "I hope you don't mind me coming on the trip."

"No of course not, why should I?"

But she didn't mean it. She knew then the holiday was going to be a disaster.

2

DREW walked across to the fire and turned looking at her with an anxious clouded look in his dark eyes as though he was trying to solve a problem and not succeeding. Maggie felt puzzled. Drew never had problems. It was other people who had those.

"You haven't changed as much as I thought you would," he said suddenly. "How old are you?"

"You should know that," she replied impatiently. "You've known me long enough."

"Yes I have," he replied slowly. "That's why I don't understand your engagement to my brother."

"I think it's obvious. Joel's a dear, sweet person."

"Can the qualities of dear and sweet sustain your interest for a

29

lifetime. I doubt it."

"Let me be the judge of that," she replied coldly, turning and looking down at the moat. It wasn't so bad the holiday was only seven days.

"I hear you've been making a name for yourself in rep."

"Joel's been exaggerating," she answered without looking round. "And the company was comparatively unknown. Anyway it's closed its doors for good so I'm now out of a job."

"That's tough luck, Maggie."

She looked round surprised to hear the note of sympathy in his voice. "The company would have stood a better chance if it had been located at Windermere or Kendal," she continued, "with a continuous stream of tourists and hikers . . . Know what I'd really like to do? Start my own company but that would be like asking for the moon."

Drew raised his eyebrows in surprise. "And what does your future husband

30

think of that." His tone was mocking, amused.

"I haven't discussed it with him yet." Maggie held her head high. Her old aunt had always told her conversation was a game of tennis. She sent a new ball back.

"How's the electronics business?"

"Couldn't be better," he said sitting on the arm of a chair. "In fact I've had quite a time rearranging my schedule so I could take a week off."

"I presume Irina's away on tour," asked Maggie looking at him curiously.

"You presume correctly."

The conversation continued for a few more minutes about the journey, what the weather would be like, whether or not they would like the country. It was in the tone of Drew's voice, the way he phrased his questions, the hard expression in his eyes that served to give an impression of suppressed anger. What is the matter with him thought Maggie, it was almost like being with a time bomb, so that when the door

31

opened and Joel and Bebe returned Maggie felt relieved.

"Joel made me take my second pair of boots out," complained Bebe petulantly. "And you know the average temperature in Moscow in November is minus ten . . . "

"One pair is enough," interrupted Joel. "For goodness' sake Bebe, we'll only be there a week."

"Pity we couldn't have booked for longer," she said with a sigh.

"You know it was impossible." Joel looked at her exasperatedly. "Anyway you'll find one week will help your Russian enormously."

Bebe had draped her long legs over the chair arm, her fingers playing with a tassel at her waist, a strand of blonde hair had fallen across her woebegone face.

"It was a mistake me doing the Russian Studies course," she said looking across at Joel. "I should have kept to history."

"Nonsense," Joel exclaimed. "A lot

of people find the first year difficult — anyway see your tutor. That's what he's there for."

Mrs Meeson had set out a cold ham salad in the dining-room and giving Joel a fierce look, apologised profusely for the lack of hot food but she had been given virtually no warning that visitors were coming. And as she served the food in the panelled dining-room at the old gate-legged table with the silver candle sticks and the portrait of Drew and Joel's mother gazing down on them, Maggie started to relax.

The food and wine improved everyone's spirits and after the second glass Bebe sparkled non-stop about Seattle and Vancouver. Drew looked interested as he studied her face across the table. Maggie looked at him. How foolish of her to think Drew was going to spoil the holiday. She was engaged to Joel, Drew was married to Irina and if Drew desired a little feminine company, what better than blonde, blue-eyed Bebe to keep him happy.

When the meal finished Drew was talking to Bebe about horticulture and took her into the conservatory to show her the orchids. Maggie turned to Joel.

"Why didn't you tell me Drew was coming?" she chided him. "He's the last person I would choose to go on holiday with."

Joel looked sheepish. "I knew there was a possibility that if you knew Drew was coming you might back out so I delayed as long as I could. I couldn't bear it if you didn't come."

"You're sweet Joel," said Maggie running her fingers through his fair curly hair. Later that evening they kissed lingeringly outside Maggie's door.

They set off the following morning in the first light of dawn. Down the long drive a light wind playfully scurried the autumn leaves, then onto the main road leading to the motorway. Drew drove, Maggie sat next to him, whilst

Joel and Bebe occupied the back seat.

They had just gone through Stratford-upon-Avon when Drew suddenly exclaimed:

"Ignition light's come on. Battery's not charging. Did you take the car to Mathesons as I said?" He looked at Joel in the driving mirror.

"Sorry, Drew. I forgot. I've been so busy."

Drew cursed under his breath. The ignition light steady on the dashboard.

"I'm turning round and going back. We'll get the Range Rover."

There was deadly silence in the car as they made the return journey, transferred themselves and luggage to the Range Rover then set off again. When they got onto the motorway to make up for lost time Drew drove at a steady seventy in the fast lane.

"Why did I agree to come?" he muttered angrily.

"Yes, why did you?" asked Maggie, giving him a quick glance.

But Drew declined to answer.

The plane for Moscow was half empty. Not surprising, thought Maggie. Not exactly the sort of place the British rush to in droves. Bebe had manoeuvred herself into the seat next to Joel whilst Maggie sat behind with Drew across the aisle. How had Bebe managed it? Must have happened at the baggage check-in when she was talking to Drew.

Drew was asleep and on his face was a tired careworn look. He's been overworking thought Maggie, that's why he's taking a week off. After a few minutes he stirred and opened his eyes, and as his gaze alighted on Maggie the sleepy look gave way to smouldering anger.

"What's the matter, Drew?" asked Maggie. "You look so angry?"

"I'm not angry," he replied. "Just depressed."

"Depressed!" she exclaimed in perplexity. She failed totally to understand him. "You're going on holiday. You should be carefree."

He made a bitter sound. "I wish I was."

Suddenly there was a sudden burst of laughter from Joel and Bebe, then Joel turned round and handed Maggie a magazine. "See page thirty," he said with a smile.

"I'm afraid I'm going to be a bit of a drag on the party." Drew looked across at Maggie as she flipped through the magazine.

"Nonsense," she said pausing to look up. "You're going to enjoy it."

"Whether I like it or not."

"Look at the page thirty joke and let's have a smile."

She handed Drew the magazine. He didn't smile. "Anti-Russian jokes are not appreciated in Russia. Leave it on the plane."

"What will make you smile."

"Seeing that freckle on your nose wrinkle up."

She rolled up the magazine and playfully hit him with it. "I haven't got a freckle on my nose."

Bebe turned round in her seat. "Maggie, how about buying a mink coat in Russia."

Maggie looked at her thoughtfully. She had always had a dream of mink and diamonds, in some glamorous setting.

Drew broke into her thoughts. "You're not the mink type."

"What type am I?" she queried coming back to earth.

He regarded her carefully, head on one side, narrowing his eyes.

"Outdoor type — skiing, climbing, swimming."

Maggie considered this for a moment. "I think you're right. Anyway I haven't got the money and I hate animals being killed for their fur. I was really thinking of an image I want to create."

"Forget that nonsense," Drew said exasperatedly. "Just be yourself." Then lowering his voice he added, "Why don't you turn your mind to more immediate matters. For example, you've got a problem with Bebe."

Immediately Maggie bristled.

"Why should I?" she asked sharply giving Drew a hard look. "Joel and I love each other."

"Are you sure?" He grimaced rising his eyebrows.

"Of course we're sure."

"Why are you getting so agitated?"

"I'm not getting agitated," she said irritably.

Drew leaned back in his seat, a slow smile spreading across his face. His tension and depression was lifting thought Maggie, but he's not doing me any good.

"Maggie," came Drew's voice.

Maggie turned her head wearily; there was a mischievous look in Drew's eyes.

"A short while ago you asked me what type you are. You're not Joel's type."

Maggie's eyes flashed and she opened her mouth to retort. It was fortunate at that moment the stewardess handed her the luncheon tray.

'Don't rise to the bait,' she told herself as she cut the bread roll and buttered it. Drew has no consideration for other people's feelings. Of course she was Joel's type. It was so obvious. They got on so well together.

"What are you going to do until you get a job?" came Drew's voice again. Maggie thought for a moment.

"I could get work in a hotel but I'd rather help Dad with the sheep."

When Drew had finished his meal he leaned back and closed his eyes and had a mental picture of Maggie tending her flock on a Cumbrian mountainside. He felt comfortable and relaxed. He always felt like this after talking to Maggie. He hadn't been sleeping well; it was those damn headaches. He really ought to see a doctor.

He must have fallen asleep again for when he awoke the second time it was twilight outside the cabin and the light on the starboard wing tip glowed in the gathering darkness. Down below lay the U.S.S.R.

40

He hoped it wouldn't be a wasted journey.

★ ★ ★

Maggie thought their party would never get through passport control. The official regarded each one of them with suspicion and appeared to read every word on their passports and visas. At length they were through; and beyond the barrier an attractive woman with a mane of long fair hair awaited them. She smiled courteously and spoke in perfect English:

"Please collect your luggage and after Customs go to the main entrance and board the Intourist bus. I shall be waiting for you."

"She'll always be waiting for us," whispered Joel to Maggie.

"Who is she?" Maggie whispered back.

"The guide/interpreter allocated to us. Also a member of the K.G.B."

"I hope you're joking."

41

They moved into the Customs hall. Here the men were subject to a rigorous search, the women being largely ignored, then walking through to the airport foyer with its low ceiling of steel cylindrical shapes and soft lighting, the waiting orange and white bus of Intourist was easily discernible outside the entrance.

Maggie took a seat by the window and Joel sat next to her.

"This is a change sitting next to me," Maggie laughed.

Joel's hand stole over hers. "Sorry we weren't together on the plane. Just the way things worked out."

"Don't give it another thought," said Maggie happy now that Joel was at her side. "I can't believe we're really in Russia. What will you do when you get your degree?"

Joel pursed his lips. "I wouldn't mind the diplomatic service."

"You mean work in an embassy. Perhaps the British Embassy in Moscow."

"If I'm lucky."

"What kind of job will Bebe get?"

"I don't think Bebe takes her studies seriously and of course she's had this emotional upset with Guy."

Maggie glanced down the bus. Bebe was in animated conversation with a middle-aged bearded man and from time to time turned to Drew, who was seated across the aisle, to place her hand on his arm and express some comment.

"I think she's almost over it," said Maggie in a cool voice.

"I'm so glad," said Joel. "Bebe's a great girl. And I'm so glad she came on this trip. She likes you."

"That's nice," replied Maggie. "Joel, there's something the matter with Drew. He looks so strained."

"Not sleeping well," replied Joel. "Sometimes I hear him get up and go out for a walk."

"In the middle of the night?"

Joel nodded. "I expect he misses Irina. She's always away."

"Is that the reason why she isn't with Drew on this trip?"

"I expect so, but Drew doesn't tell me much. I'm just the kid brother."

The bus swung out onto the main highway for Moscow. The guide/interpreter stood up, microphone in hand.

"Welcome to Russia. My name is Greisha," she paused and smiled. "It is my job to see you have a holiday without problems but it is prudent of me to warn you of pitfalls for the foreign visitor. For example you may only take photographs of buildings of cultural interest. You may only exchange your foreign currency at a State Bank or a Bureau de Change at your hotel. It is an offence to exchange with private individuals . . . "

The list was endless. Maggie stared through the window into the inky darkness. What would Russia bring for her? A closening of her relationship with Joel, a strengthening of the bond. Suddenly Greisha broke into her thoughts.

" . . . During the next few days we are going to visit many places of great interest. The circus, we have the best circus in the world. The ballet, we have the best ballet in the world. The U.S.S.R. Exhibition of Economic Achievements . . . "

"We've got them there," whispered Joel.

"Ssh!" whispered Maggie.

The bus had now entered Moscow and from the window she caught glimpses of enormous empty squares, big enough to take a battalion of soldiers. The evening rush had finished and traffic was light, or was it always light?

The bus stopped outside a modern hotel in Gorki Street. At the entrance stood an armed policeman in his dark grey overcoat and black fur hat.

"Why do they have armed police?" asked Bebe as they entered through the swing doors.

"Stop private citizens getting in and seeing the goodies ladled out

45

to foreigners like you and me," Joel grinned at her.

Everyone looked tired. At the reception desk everyone handed over their passports and visas and in return were handed their hotel pass which bore their room number. At the key counter they collected their keys on production of the hotel pass, then up in the lift to the nineteenth floor.

A few yards from the lift entrance was seated the floor lady. She was a homely-looking woman, elderly, tired, but polite. She was dressed in a faded overall of the type Maggie remembered her grandmother wearing. On her desk a card announced 'Morning Tea 6 kopeks, Service charge 2 kopeks.' At 100 kopeks to the rouble and 1 rouble to the pound it was a bargain. Maggie couldn't resist ordering. The woman did not speak English and Joel came to her rescue.

"*Chai. Smalakom. Spasiba*," instructed Joel, then turning to Maggie. "Show her your key number."

The matter of the tea settled they continued down the softly carpeted corridor. Joel paused at his door, gave Maggie a kiss on the cheek, his arm straying around her waist.

"Good night, darling. I feel all in. Sleep well."

"Good night, Joel. See you tomorrow."

"Good night," called Bebe from across the corridor. "Gee I'm glad I came. It's like being in a movie. I wouldn't have missed it for anything."

Maggie continued down the corridor following Drew. His room was opposite hers.

"Can't say I echo Bebe's sentiments," he remarked acidly pausing at his door.

"You'll be coming on the sight-seeing tours?" asked Maggie inserting the key in her door.

"Not if I can help it," he replied. "Good night, Maggie."

"Good night."

She turned the key and opened the door. It was a pleasing room panelled in dark wood, 'L' shaped with a sleeping and sitting area. Flopping into an armchair by the television Maggie looked at the double top sheet with a diamond-shaped opening through which the chambermaid had stuffed a blanket.

She was thinking of Drew. He was certainly behaving in an odd manner. And her mind strayed back through the years to a Sunday of sharp frost and sunshine. It was long before he met Irina and he had asked her to go for a walk. She hadn't wanted to go, she would have rather spent the afternoon with Joel cleaning up the pigeon loft over the stables. But he had persuaded her and she had gone.

They had walked along a tributary of the Kingsley River, wading through the water at shallow levels because Drew had spotted some unusual bird on the far bank. Then they had had the most extraordinary luck and seen a heron, who at their approach had risen into the air with the slow beat of its great wings. It had been quite a thrill, herons are so rare. Maggie had started to enjoy herself and when they got to the village Drew had suggested tea at the 'Copper Kettle'. And as she sat there relaxed and contented, she had a vision of a world that was a soft gentle place. Then suddenly Drew had flared up, criticising her harshly over some trivial incident, and the vision had been shattered.

Maggie got up from her chair and started to undress. Drew had spoilt that day as he had spoilt so many. Well, he wasn't going to spoil this holiday. She took her toilet bag out of her case and went into the bathroom. She was still thinking of Drew. If he had no intention of going on sight-seeing tours why had he come to Russia at all?

3

ABOUT half-past seven the following morning Maggie was awakened by a tap on the door. It was the floor lady, a shy smile on her homely face.

"*Dobraye utra*," she greeted Maggie. She was carrying a tray and on the white embroidered tray cloth stood a white china cup and saucer, stainless-steel teapot, and a sugar basin.

"Thank you," said Maggie. "*Spasiba*." She took the tray from her and closed the door. There was no milk but the tea tasted surprisingly pleasant without it, then walking across to the window she drew back the curtains and took her first look at Moscow in the daylight.

She was looking down on early nineteenth-century buildings, four storeys high. They had that elegant Regency look, with the exteriors painted cream and gold, and in the narrow street that ran between the buildings, Russians in their dark winter coats and fur hats with a chilled expression on their faces were hurrying to work.

The city was so quiet, it was almost uncanny. Was it always like this? Then with a tingle of excitement she remembered from the travel brochure that the Kremlin and Red Square were only a few minutes walk away. Maggie's foreign travel had been sadly neglected — one school trip to France and a long weekend in Brussels. Most of her holidays had been spent in Scotland visiting relations.

She stepped into a long thick tweed skirt, then pulled a floppy green sweater over her head, wondering what today would bring.

Drew was going off on his own and she would be in a threesome with Joel and Bebe. She felt a sense of irritation then immediately felt ashamed. Of course Joel had insisted that Bebe should come on the holiday, just the sort of thing he would do, helping a damsel in distress, and she was being petty and mean-spirited. She resolved to be extra nice to Bebe.

Still, it was a pity Drew would not be going sight-seeing with them she thought pushing her feet into a pair of warm boots and zipping them up, at least it would have made the threesome into a foursome, which from Maggie's point of view would have been far more satisfactory. Why did Drew have to be so difficult? A leopard can't change his spots, thought Maggie, as she picked up her shoulder bag and opened the door.

What was he going to do today, she thought, as she walked down the softly lit corridor. Wander round Moscow alone? To her knowledge he did not speak Russian and in a country where activities which are regarded as legal in the United Kingdom, are treated as a punishable offence, it could be an intimidating experience. She shrugged her shoulders. There was nothing she could do.

Passing Joel's door she decided to knock. He opened it with a sleepy look on his face.

"Come in, Maggie," he said yawning. "I'm tired."

"Why's that?" she asked walking into a room where the contents of his case appeared to have been flung across the room. The television was on — a documentary on collective farming. Joel switched the set off.

"That's one part of the system that doesn't work."

"Didn't you sleep well last night?" she asked as Joel gave another yawn.

"Didn't sleep enough. Got to bed sometime after two, then the floor lady brought me tea at seven. She must have got her wires crossed. The tea was only for you. Did you get yours by the way?"

"Yes, thanks. What were you doing until two this morning?"

A look of embarrassment came over

his face. "Look, Maggie, I phoned your room, I even went down and knocked, but you must have been out like a light. You see Bebe got this idea of seeing Red Square by moonlight."

Maggie kept her voice calm. "Did you enjoy it?"

"Unforgettable." He picked up his jacket and opened the door. Bebe was standing there.

"Hey, Maggie. Pity we couldn't waken you last night but you really missed something."

"So it seems."

They started walking down the corridor to the lift, Maggie struggling with a green-eyed monster. She knew if she tried hard enough she'd succeed.

"Where's Drew?" asked Bebe as they entered the lift, Bebe squeezing between them. She was wearing a black sweater that was so tight it must have shrunk in the wash.

"I'm giving Drew a wide berth at the moment," Maggie replied with a grin.

"He's not exactly the happiest man on the tour."

"Perhaps he's got financial problems," Bebe suggested.

The lift zoomed down to the third floor where breakfast was being served in a room with a low wooden ceiling painted crimson and decorated with small white flowers. Samovars stood on sideboards, framed pictures of log cabins on lakeshores, and people dressed in furs riding in troikas through the snow decorated the walls.

One almost expected to hear the balalaika as young male waiters served bread and cheese, currant buns and fried eggs, to the tour guests seated at four long tables. Joel sat opposite Maggie looking terribly English in his Harris tweed. Drew hadn't put in an appearance.

"I think I'm suffering from culture shock," said Bebe taking a bite into a currant bun. "I guess I'll stay in the hotel this morning."

"The after-effects of Red Square at

midnight?" asked Maggie not unkindly.

"I guess so," replied Bebe. "You see there was this flame symbolising the spirit of Russia and we must have walked too close to it or something, I'm not sure, because suddenly a soldier blew his whistle and a whole lot of them came running and we were surrounded. Was I scared! I thought my God, we're going to be sent to Siberia."

"They wouldn't have done that," interjected Joel with a smile. "Tourists are valuable people with lots of hard currency to spend."

"What happened then?" asked Maggie wide-eyed with curiosity.

"Oh they just gestured to us to move on, which we certainly did."

The middle-aged bearded man Maggie had seen Bebe talking to on the bus the previous evening leaned across.

"I couldn't help overhearing your remark about hard currency. It is of tremendous importance to them because there is such a great demand for goods from the west." Then turning to Bebe he said with a smile, "You had nothing to fear last night. They couldn't make a court case out of standing too close to the sacred flame. But don't let it happen again."

"I certainly won't," replied Bebe. "Gee I wish I knew a lot about Russia. You see I've started this course . . . "

"What is the most important thing that has happened here this century?" the bearded man interrupted.

Bebe hesitated. "I think they had a revolution."

The bearded man looked pleased. "Correct and it took place in Leningrad. Now what do you know of Napoleon?"

Bebe looked worried. "He retreated from Moscow in eighteen-twelve. I read it on the sleeve of a record."

"Correct. Napoleon entered a deserted Moscow on the morning of the fourteenth September eighteen-twelve. That evening for reasons which have never been fully explained, the city caught fire. It burned for six days until heavy rains extinguished the flames.

Now a great deal of food had been burnt in the fire and it became clear to Napoleon that the remaining stocks would not last until the spring. There was only one thing to do, send a peace proposal to the Czar . . . "

"You a history teacher or something . . . ?" Bebe interrupted.

"I used to teach history," replied the man. "By the way, my name is Collins."

"I'm Bebe. Bebe Rossenburg and these are my friends Maggie and Joel."

Mr Collins nodded to them. "Pleased to meet you. Now if you will excuse me . . . "

Mr Collins got up and walked across the room. At the entrance he passed Drew who hurried across and took an empty seat next to Maggie. He smelt of some spicy aftershave and looked warm and snug in a white polo neck.

"You just missed a history lesson," said Joel passing him the coffee pot.

"On what? Russia?"

Joel nodded.

"Sorry I missed it. Always glad to learn a little more about this extraordinary country. I've just met Greisha. It's Red Square this morning and the Intourist bus is waiting now."

He seemed in better spirits as if the problem he had had yesterday had been solved or was about to be solved. Maggie looked across at him curiously.

"I take it you're not coming," she asked knowing the answer and for some obscure reason wanting to probe.

"That's right. This egg's cold. Ghastly." He pushed the plate way.

"Exploring alone?" asked Joel.

"You could say that." Drew's voice was casual as he buttered a slice of dark brown bread and placed a piece of cheese on top.

"There are a lot of advantages going to these places with Greisha," Joel persisted. "You'll learn far more."

"I'm not here to learn," Drew rasped out.

Everyone got up. Bebe gave him an impish grin, her blue eyes laughing.

59

"Making contact with the K.G.B. by any chance?"

"If I were, I wouldn't tell you," he retorted sharply.

Bebe caught up with Maggie and Joel at the lift.

"On second thoughts I'll come with you this morning," Maggie tried to look pleased. "I'm glad you've changed your mind," she said as they stepped into the lift.

"Why is Drew so unsociable?" asked Bebe as the lift glided noiselessly down to the ground floor. "He's like a bear with a sore head."

"I've been asking myself that question for a long time," answered Joel.

In the forecourt of the hotel they boarded the Intourist bus and ten minutes later set off through the great squares, Manege, Sverdlov and Revolution, radiating fanlike from west to east, so enormous they made London squares look small and toylike.

The bus stopped a hundred yards or so from Red Square, and as everyone

60

got out an incredible sight met their eyes. In the foreground stood St Basil's Cathedral with its onion-shaped domes, red and white striped and yellow and green intertwirling, so utterly oriental, and beyond Red Square, where the high red brick crenellated wall of the Kremlin stood.

They started walking across the square, the wind stinging like a whip. From time to time large black American style limousines drove out of the Kremlin entrance with grey-faced men seated in the back, past the never-ending queue of pilgrims to the tomb of Lenin, whilst high above the Kremlin wall the red flag shivered in the wind.

Changing of the guard commenced, the soldiers doing high goose steps.

"My God," exclaimed Bebe. "How this country makes my blood run cold."

"Yesterday you said it was like being in a movie," Maggie reminded her.

"That was yesterday," Bebe replied dolefully.

"What made you choose Russian

61

Studies?" Maggie continued.

"Why do we do crazy things? To think I could have chosen French and be in Paris right now."

The celebrations of the October Revolution had recently taken place and stout elderly women in dark coats and white headscarves were busy dismantling decorations, taking away bunches of red flowers and sweeping the square with large brooms.

Greisha spoke to the party. "In Russian 'red' means 'beautiful'. That is why our most important and attractive square is called red." The party moved off following Greisha. Bebe moved off with them.

"As much as I like Bebe it's nice to have a break," smiled Joel watching her retreating fur-clad figure. "That woman's beginning to haunt me."

"I've seen the way she looks at you," Maggie teased. "You shouldn't be so devastating to the opposite sex."

"I wish I had that effect on you," he grasped her hand. "Sometimes you

62

seem so distant, so remote. Maggie, what about getting married next month? We'll make it a Christmas wedding. I'll move out of college hall and get a flat in town. Saw a nice one the other day, fully furnished, fitted kitchen, shower room . . ."

"Not so fast Joel. Other things have to be considered."

Joel's shining eyes clouded. "Such as?"

"Well there's Dad."

"What about him?"

"He's in trouble — financial trouble. Just before I left I saw a letter from his bank. I can't just walk out on him — not just yet."

"How long will that be?"

"I don't know, Joel. Six months, a year — I don't know."

"Is this a gentle way of letting me down? Giving me the push?"

"Of course it isn't," she replied fiercely. "Oh Joel, you've placed me in such a difficult position. I do love you, really I do."

63

"Of course you do," he said patting her hand. "Come on let's join the others."

When they got back to their hotel Maggie went up to her room. Her conversation with Joel troubled her. She thought of the wedding Joel had suggested next month and the cramped flat in the provincial town, and was filled with a sense of claustrophobia as she lay on the bed her chin cupped in her hands. And what about her stage career? It hadn't even been discussed. That obviously would come to an end unless they agreed to live apart most of the time. Yet she knew Joel would make a wonderful husband. They'd have to work something out, a plan that would suit both their needs.

At lunch Maggie listened to Bebe's account of her childhood on Long Island with a deflated sense of having let Joel down. Joel was busy talking to a librarian from Brixton. She had a feeling he was avoiding conversational contact. She didn't blame him, it was all her fault. Then suddenly he turned and smiled at her and she was happy.

"How do you like the caviar?" he asked.

"I like the Chicken Kiev better," she replied putting her fork into the chicken breast and hot melted butter oozing out.

"How about the circus tonight and the ballet tomorrow night?" Bebe suggested leaning her arms on the table. "I think it's the Bolshoi."

"Great idea," said Joel. "What do you say Maggie?"

"I'm in agreement."

"That's nice for a change." He gave her a meaningful look.

"What about Drew?" asked Bebe. "Shall I get him tickets. I see he hasn't shown up for lunch." She glanced around the tables.

Joel looked doubtful. "Drew seems to be keen on going it alone."

"We've got to book the seats now," said Bebe. "Otherwise we won't go at all. Do I get him a ticket for

65

each show?" She looked at Joel for an answer.

"Yes, go ahead, and if he doesn't want to come we can always sell them. On second thoughts he'll definitely go to the ballet. After all he is married to a ballet dancer."

Bebe's eyes opened wide. "You don't say. Which company is she in?"

"Royal Westminster, I think."

"Royal Westminster!" Bebe exclaimed delighted. "I saw them in New York last year and thought they were terrific! What's her name?"

"Irina Doestraskaya."

"He's married to a Russian girl!" Bebe looked surprised.

"She's British," Maggie put in. "It's her father who was Russian. He arrived in England at the end of the last war, — a refugee; he'd been in a German P.O.W. camp. He decided to make this country his home, became a naturalised British subject and married an Englishwoman."

"Gee, what a story," exclaimed Bebe.

She rose to her feet. "I'm definitely staying in the hotel this afternoon and writing a lot of letters back home. See you tonight."

They watched Bebe's slim figure saunter out of the dining-room.

"There's a tour leaving in a few minutes for the Kremlin." Joel turned to Maggie giving her a soft smile. "Like to come?"

"Love to. Joel, about this morning, I'm really sorry . . . "

"Forget it."

The Kremlin bus was travelling down Marx Prospekt, and Maggie, seated next to Joel was gazing contentedly through the window admiring the smart Moscow women in their black boots, black leather coats trimmed with silver fox and silver fox hats. She felt so relaxed in Joel's company. There was a lot to be said for that. No sharp criticisms, no angry retorts. She could have a very pleasant life with Joel, when suddenly the bus stopped at the traffic lights.

Two men were walking along the pavement near the bus, deep in conversation. One was short, thick set, wearing a brown leather coat and fur hat, the other was Drew! There was no mistaking him in his English sheepskin, white polo neck sweater and bare-headed.

To her knowledge Drew knew no one in Moscow!

4

THE lights changed and the bus moved off. Maggie turned to Joel.

"Did you see that!" she exclaimed, a perplexed expression on her face. "Drew talking to a man by the traffic lights."

Joel couldn't refrain from laughing. "What's so extraordinary about that. Russians love talking to English visitors. They usually end up by asking to buy some item of your clothing. Last time I came they were stopping me all the time. The 'House of Books' is a good place. You get Russian undergrads hanging around there all the time waiting to have a conversation to improve their English."

"This man wasn't a student — he was middle-aged."

Joel patted Maggie's hand. "Forget it. Drew's a big boy; he can look after himself. Anyway, why so interested in Drew? What about me? I asked you to marry me next month and I've been put off."

"I've told you about Dad. I can't just leave him right now, he's all I've got."

Joel leaned towards her. "You've got me," he said softly.

Maggie slipped her hand into his. "Yes, I've got you Joel," she whispered and she felt a warm glow inside her filling her with contentment.

The bus stopped and they all got out, following Greisha in her red coat and the rest of the tour party. The walls of the Kremlin loomed before them, high and secret, interspersed with towers and gateways like a prison.

They entered through the Spassky Gate. Maggie was pleasantly surprised, it was much better inside. It seemed to be a miniature town of cathedrals, palaces, and officials buildings with golden domes and spires carrying red stars.

"The Kremlin means fortress," came Greisha's slow perfect pronunciation, "and was founded in the twelfth century. Today it is the workplace of the Soviet leadership. Observe the white lines, you are not allowed to step beyond . . ."

Who was the man Drew was talking to in the Marx Prospekt thought Maggie as they followed Greisha across the square.

They were talking together in an earnest manner and obviously knew each other well. What exactly did Drew do in electronics? Wasn't it research and development, and wasn't he a key person in his department. She wished she'd paid more attention when Joel had been chatting about him.

Joel slipped his arm through hers. "I'm glad Bebe decided not to come. I can have you all to myself for the afternoon."

Drew slipped from her mind and she turned her full attention to Joel.

"You always say the nicest things."

Joel grinned. "When you lived at Kingsley Magna I was always saying the nicest things but you never seemed to notice."

She smiled gently at him. It was true she thought. He had always been there unnoticed in the wings. It was just that it had taken her a long time to grow up. They entered the Cathedral of the Assumption. What a dazzle of chandeliers, shrines of bronze and silver, doors plated with black-lacquered copper with biblical themes in gold, the icon wall of holy paintings encrusted with precious stones. They strolled in hushed silence from one art treasure to the next.

Leaving the cathedral door, the icy wind of Moscow buffeted them across the square to the next cathedral. Joel's eyes were upon Maggie.

"Is next month totally out of the question?" he whispered.

"Give me a bit of time." She smiled gently at him. "Try to be patient."

"I'll try."

How different the two brothers were she thought as they entered the next cathedral. With Drew one had always felt some crisis was looming round the corner. Life would never be like that with Joel, she thought happily. Life with Joel would be all plain sailing.

"What are you thinking about?" Joel asked as they paused before an icon.

"Something nice about you," she replied with a smile.

"That's encouraging, but remember my patience is not unlimited."

When the tour was completed they got back into the bus. Joel sat staring ahead deep in thought.

"What's the problem, Joel?"

"It's Drew," he said at length. "He's got something on his mind. I tried prising him once or twice but it didn't work. I was astonished when he said he wanted to come with us to Russia. Not really his scene. He's never shown any interest in Russia before."

They climbed the steps to the hotel entrance and entered through the swing doors past the armed policeman.

"Why don't you talk to him?" Maggie suggested. "You're his brother."

Joel gave a hard laugh. "That doesn't mean much. It wouldn't help if I was a casual friend. Drew's a very private kind of person."

Maggie went up to her room to change for the circus. She was looking forward to it. She hadn't seen the clowns and acrobats since she was a child, except on television and she didn't count that.

She took the dress she had bought at Kendal out of the wardrobe. It was her favourite colour, deep turquoise with a wide full skirt and large white collar. She slipped into it, then opened the zipped section of her handbag where she had put a few items of jewellery and selected a silver bracelet. She hadn't worn it for years. The design was a lacy pattern, delicate and attractive and as she put it on her wrist and secured the fastener a memory flared up and reeled at her.

She had been wearing the bracelet the day Drew had tried to seduce her.

It was a memory she thought she had successfully submerged deep in her subconscious but there it was mocking and humiliating her. Suddenly she was no longer in a Moscow hotel but in a field bordering Kingsley Wood, late afternoon of a summer's day with the smell of cut grass drying in the sun. It was her last day at Kingsley Magna. She had just left Drama School, got the job at Lazonby, and the following morning she and her father would be leaving to start a new life in Cumbria. It was a feeling like being suspended in space. She had gone out into the fields, and being a sunny day had lain down in the long grass, closing her eyes, feeling the warmth of the sun on her body. She was just drifting off into a state of semi-consciousness when a small sound disturbed her and she had opened her eyes to see Drew standing over her. She had sat up, rubbing her eyes in surprise and Drew had sat down next to her, his expression serious and tension in his voice.

"Where've you been hiding yourself?" he had demanded. "I've been looking for you everywhere."

Then he had started talking about the estate and his father's health. She had only been half listening for Drew's finger was slowly running up and down her bare arm given her a peculiar shivering sensation. Then suddenly she was in his arms and his hands were running over her thighs and stomach, his lips burning into hers. He was like a man with a ravenous hunger.

She had managed to break away and move into a kneeling position.

"Have you taken leave of your senses?" she had demanded angrily.

"No." He had given her a slow enigmatic smile. "Just coming to them." Then he had sat up and grasped her hand. "Don't go tomorrow," he had implored. "Stay here."

"And why should I do that?"

He had pulled her to him and she

had fallen on top of him as his fingers had felt her breasts through the thin fabric of her dress. Then suddenly his fingers had found her nipples and she had hit him across the face. He had not flinched, but gazed steadfastly into her eyes.

"I'm going too fast for you, Maggie. You see, I want you so badly."

Then he had gathered her into his arms again, soothing with gentle words, kissing her eyes, her nose, her throat. Then the hand that was on her knee started moving in an upward direction. Struggling, trembling, somehow she had disengaged herself from Drew's embrace and got to her feet.

"Don't be scared Maggie," he had said looking up at her. "Be a good girl and sit down." He patted the grass next to him.

"Does Irina know you're here?" she asked, trying to keep her voice calm, controlled.

"What's it got to do with Irina?"

She had turned and started hurrying

across the fields, a choking sensation in her throat, the sound of Drew's voice in her ears.

"Come back, Maggie. You little fool."

She hadn't stopped until she had reached their cottage. He was marrying Irina. All he wanted her for was a plaything, a mistress. It was the final insult.

She took the bracelet off and put it back into her bag, her hand trembling slightly, and despite the warmth of the room she suddenly felt cold. Bebe was leaving Drew's ticket for the circus with Greisha. She hoped he wouldn't turn up.

She brushed her hair and glossed her lips. Next week she would be back in Cumbria so what was she worrying about. At dinner she sat between Joel and Bebe. A sombre mood had settled over her and she was starting to have a guilty feeling about her career. She had no business really going on this holiday. She should be in London going round the agents trying to get fixed up with some more auditions.

"Something wrong, Maggie?" asked Joel, perceptive as always looking at her with concern in his eyes.

Maggie put on a brave smile. "Not really. Just trying to work out what I do when we get back."

"What do you do back in England?" Bebe asked passing a dish of ice cream to her.

"I'm an actress — resting at the moment."

Bebe looked interested. "There was a time when I wanted to act. Have I seen you in anything?"

"Not unless you've been to the wilds of Cumbria."

It started to snow as they set off, and in the light of the street lamps — lamps which were sprays of white globular lights fanning out between the tall silver birches, large slowly falling flakes shone before they touched the ground.

The circus was housed in a circular

tent-like building of stone and glass, and as they entered through one of the many doors all corridors were crowded with eagerly anticipating adults and children.

At a barrier everyone had to hand over their hats and coats, and an old man with a sad deeply lined face like a character from Dostoyevsky handed them a numbered tag. Maggie, Joel and Bebe took their seats in the enormous circular auditorium whilst high on their right the circus orchestra played lively Russian dances. There was a false gaiety about Bebe. She laughed too hard at Joel's mild jokes and sat with her hands clenched. Then the lights dimmed and five video films started — patriotic films of soldiers marching, flags waving, crowds smiling, tanks rolling, and over it all an excited male voice extolling the glories of Russia.

It began to be too much for Maggie. "We ought to go to the circus and have someone tell us about the glories of Great Britain," she exclaimed with feeling to Joel and Bebe. "The Battle of Britain, the North African campaign . . ."

"Steady on," intervened Joel but Maggie couldn't stop.

" . . . and Nelson at Trafalgar, and Wellington at Waterloo."

Maggie held her head high, her eyes shining, her voice full of emotion.

"Gee I'd love to see you in a play," exclaimed Bebe. "I bet you're terrific. Don't you think so, Joel? Don't you think Maggie's going to be a great actress?"

Joel looked unconcerned. "Maggie's talents lie in other directions," he said coolly. "And her first duty will be to be a good wife."

Maggie had often wondered what Joel thought of her acting career, and now he had said it. She felt an overwhelming sense of disappointment. She was glad when the show started, when the pool of light lit the circus ring and the acts began.

It was when the trapeze artists were

81

giving a marvellous impression of space walking that Maggie knew the empty seat next to her had been taken. There was the sudden smell of spicy aftershave, the rough feel of his tweed jacket against her arm.

The act finished, the lights came on and Maggie turned and looked at him — Drew's face looked grey. He was a man with a lot of worry.

"I didn't think you were coming at all," she said evenly.

"Neither did I," he replied unsmilingly.

He was wearing a grey tweed suit, looked expensive, with a paler grey shirt. Why didn't Joel dress like that instead of that casual gear all the time.

"I saw you talking to a man in Marx Prospekt this afternoon."

Drew's face remained immobile.

"I didn't know you had friends in Moscow."

Drew's silence was now irritating.

"Well I hope you know what you're doing," she said sharply.

Drew swung into action. "And what are you implying? Something nasty? I'm ashamed of you. My father was a naval officer all through the last war . . . "

"Well, why don't you explain yourself?"

"Why should I?"

"Oh do what the hell you want!"

"Hey you two, save the fight till afterwards." Joel looked across at Drew. "Thought you weren't coming. Where've you been?"

"Sight-seeing."

"In the dark?" asked Bebe, gurgling with laughter.

Drew grinned at her. "You see another kind of Moscow at night."

"I'll bet," she laughed.

Drew ignored this innuendo. "Had a good time today?" he asked looking at Joel. Joel nodded contentedly looking at Maggie.

"Red Square and the Kremlin. You ought to see it. Bebe's going tomorrow. Why don't you join her party?"

Drew lowered his eyelids giving Bebe a flirtatious look. "I might," he smiled.

"That would be great," she exclaimed, her gold ear-rings shaking, her eyes shining.

"Then on the other hand I might not."

Bebe's mouth fell into a pouting expression and she looked away. He could always twist women around his little finger, thought Maggie, but not me. I'm one step ahead of him all the time.

"What's the matter, Maggie? Got some problem on your mind?" Drew's voice pulsed into her ear.

"No, I've solved it," she replied. Drew's eyes narrowed as he looked at her profile.

"Enigmatic as usual," he said, a weary tone in his voice.

The circus continued but the lovely glow of excited wonder had left Maggie, now that Drew was at her side, ruffling her placid waters. She turned her attention to the circus. The ring had now disappeared and in its place was an ice rink where a bevy of beautiful girls skated idyllically around the rink. Then this disappeared and a swimming-pool appeared full of bathing beauties breaking the surface like the petals of a flower. Finally the show came to an end and the audience prepared to leave.

"What do you say to a meal at the Karbatuk?" Drew suggested unexpectedly as they collected their hats and coats. "It's not far from the hotel."

"I'd love that," exclaimed Bebe. "I'm ravenous."

The Karbatuk was crowded with late night diners, seated beneath the stained-glass windows, the brass lamps, the carpets on the walls. There was a small space for dancing. As a waiter showed them to a table a pianist and violinist were playing 'Orchi Chornya'.

"The only Russian song I know is 'The Volga Boatman'," said Bebe picking up the menu. Then her expression turned to one of dismay. "It's in Russian."

"I've often wondered how you got on the Russian course," said Joel with a mischievous smile. "Here, give it to me, I'll help you. It's Oriental Russian if that makes you feel any better. I went in one of these places on my last trip. *Golubtsy* is chopped meat and rice cooked in vine leaves. Not bad. Or you could have *Narkurma* — that's lamb roast with pomegranates. For wine I suggest *Shamkhor*."

"I like the sound of roast lamb with pomegranates," said Bebe. "What do you think Maggie and Drew?"

"I rather fancy *golubtsy*," smiled Maggie.

"I'll have the same," said Drew.

The order was given then the waiter brought the wine to the table. Joel raised his glass. "Here's to our Russian holiday. May it be unforgettable."

The four of them raised their glasses and drank the toast. Then suddenly Bebe's eyes were shining with tears.

"It'll be that all right," she said brittly.

"What's happened?" asked Joel looking at her carefully. "This afternoon you said you were going to write letters."

"I did," she replied unhappily. "I started this letter to Guy and then I thought, gee, I'd love to talk to him, so I phoned. What an idiot I was." The tears started rolling down her pretty face. "You see I thought it was just a temporary thing, a lover's tiff. He's got someone else and he never wants to see me again. They're getting married."

She covered her face with her hands and howled. Joel put his arm around her shoulders.

"There now. You'll feel better after a good cry."

"I am sorry, Bebe," said Maggie. "You've had a rotten time. But the world's a big place full of nice eligible men . . ."

"Have another drink," Joel suggested.

"I think I will."

Joel refilled her glass.

"I'm sorry I'm spoiling your evening," she said looking across at Drew and

87

Maggie. "But I just couldn't help it when Joel said . . . "

The pianist and violinist struck up a quickstep.

"Like to dance?" asked Joel, his face full of compassion for Bebe's suffering.

"Gee, I'd love to."

She sauntered onto the floor, her arm went around neck, her cheek to his.

"Poor Bebe," murmured Drew over his wine. "She's having a hard time but I'm sure my brother will help soften the blow."

More couples had joined them on the floor and Bebe's head was now resting on Joel's shoulder. She looked as though she was still crying.

"Like to dance," asked Drew.

They moved onto the floor, Drew holding her at a respectful distance.

"Now don't look so worried. Joel will comfort her."

"That's what I'm worried about," said Maggie as they glided round the floor. Try as she may, she did not like it one bit. She had this feeling Joel was being manipulated.

"We have to be philosophical about these things," said Drew smiling at Maggie's worried countenance. "Life is all about making decisions so the ones who make the right ones come out on top."

"And of course you make the right decisions," she replied tartly.

To her surprise a dejected look came over his face. "No Maggie, I do not." Then he made an effort to be more cheerful and she felt his fingers tightened on her waist. "You're a good dancer," he complimented her. "Good sense of rhythm and balance."

"Thanks," she said in a flat voice. Both of Bebe's arms were now around Joel's neck.

"Forget Joel," Drew whispered. "He won't do you any good."

"I make my own decisions thank you," she replied tossing her head. Drew puzzled her. Why had he come to Russia? She looked up into his face.

"You don't go on any of the tours."

"I came to the circus tonight, didn't I?"

"I mean during the day. What are you up to?"

"Why so interested in what I do?" he whispered close to her ear.

"Oh forget it," she retorted, her cheeks flushing angrily.

They returned to the table where the waiter had arrived with their *golubtsy*. They sat down and started eating, Drew refilling Maggie's glass.

"The man I was talking to in Marx Prospekt was the administrative director of the Homsomol Theatre. I met him by chance in the National Bar. You meet everyone there sooner or later. Satisfied?"

Maggie shrugged her shoulders. "I suppose so," she replied casually. "Didn't know you were interested in theatre admin. The *golubtsy*'s not too bad."

"I had met him previously in London," Drew replied looking at

Maggie over his wine glass. "When his company were over there on a cultural exchange. He's a friend of Irina's, so stop being so damn suspicious."

"Why should I be suspicious?" asked Maggie with an air of mock innocence. It was unusual to get Drew nettled.

"Because I know you. You get a bee in your bonnet about something and you won't leave it alone. Now just forget the whole matter."

"Don't worry. I will."

Joel and Bebe returned to the table. Bebe looked as though she was trying to keep awake as she sat with her chin resting on her hands, her eyes half closed.

"Come on, Bebe," Joel urged. "You've got to eat your *Narkurma*."

"I'm not hungry anymore," she drawled in a sleepy voice.

"Pity Irina isn't here," said Joel. "She loves Oriental Russian food."

"Why isn't Irina on this trip," asked Maggie, fixing Drew with a steely gaze.

"If you don't mind," replied Drew in an irritated voice, "I don't wish to discuss Irina."

"Why ever not? She's your wife."

Drew glared at her. "Leave me alone Maggie," he rasped, an expression of utter exasperation on his face.

"I'll do just that," she flung back angrily. "And I think it's time we went back to the hotel."

They left the restaurant and started walking the empty pavements back to the hotel. The freezing temperature seemed to revive Bebe and in the distance a clock chimed midnight.

"This place is dead!" she exclaimed vehemently. "You should see New York at midnight — gee, the place is humming, everywhere's so noisy and crowded. You know it's hard to believe this is our second day in the U.S.S.R. and nothing's happened."

"Of course nothing's happened," exclaimed Joel. "What did you expect?"

"Something," she replied in a disappointed voice. "I haven't seen all those spy movies for nothing. Do you think my room's bugged?"

"Haven't a clue," laughed Joel. "But if it worries you run the bath every time you want to talk to someone."

"What a good idea!"

As soon as they got inside the hotel Drew bid them a curt goodnight and stalked off to the lifts.

"What's the matter with Drew?" exclaimed Bebe. "Have I said something?"

"Probably." Joel stifled a yawn. "I'm tired. I think I'll turn in. What do you say, Maggie?"

"Me too."

The lift took them up to the nineteenth floor and when Bebe reached her room she blew Joel a kiss before entering. It was the look of smug satisfaction on Joel's face that did it and as he lingered outside Maggie's door, his arm around her waist, Maggie could feel a hot anger building up. It had been humiliating enough watching Bebe drooling over him in the restaurant without watching kiss blowing action in the hotel.

"Let me come in," he whispered urgently. "Just for a short while."

"Now that Bebe isn't here I get your full attention," she said in a tight voice.

"Don't be like that, Maggie."

"You could have played it a little cooler," she persisted.

"For goodness' sake I only danced with her. Look Maggie, I feel a bit guilty about Bebe. You see I knew Guy was going around with someone else. I should have warned her."

"Quite a lot goes on at your college, behind the scenes — amazing any work gets done."

"Don't be like that, Maggie."

He kissed her hard on the mouth. She did not respond standing like a wooden figure. Joel realising he was wasting his time decided to cut his losses.

"Look Maggie, I'll see you tomorrow. Sleep well."

Then he turned and walked away down the corridor. As Maggie entered her room the phone started ringing. It was Drew.

"Hello, Maggie. Is Joel there?"

"No he is not," she retorted sharply.

"All right, I only asked. Look, I must talk to you. I'm in the Tea Room on the tenth floor."

All she wanted to do was curl up and sleep, but it was the unusual urgent tone in his voice that made her say:

"I'll come right away."

5

THE Tea Room was small and rectangular and made of pine. Even the tables and benches were pine with the usual samovar presiding over each table and on the walls hung white cloths embroidered in red silk.

The room was empty save for Drew seated at the furthest table from the door. As Maggie sat down opposite him a young waitress placed two cups of tea before them with slivers of lemon in a dish and a bowl of sugar. She helped herself to the sugar then looked into Drew's anxious face.

"What's the trouble, Drew?"

He gave a big sigh. "It's where to start."

"Start at the beginning," she said giving him an encouraging smile.

"The Royal Westminster Ballet is in

Moscow," he announced with an air of depression.

"You mean — Irina's in Moscow!" Maggie couldn't keep the surprise from her voice. "So that was the sudden interest in coming to Russia. I might have guessed. But you don't seem pleased."

"I'm not," he snapped. "I understand Bebe's booked tickets for the show tomorrow night. I'm not going and I've told Mr Collins he can have my ticket."

"What on earth's the matter, Drew?" She gazed at him in utter astonishment. "Irina will be upset when she hears you didn't go."

Drew did not answer. His eyes had a hard bitter look in them. Maggie sipped her lemon tea. They'd obviously had a recent quarrel. Well it was none of her business.

"Julie Harris is still with the company," she continued as though nothing was wrong. "It will be nice to see her again. We always keep in touch at

Christmas — a card and a letter giving each other the year's news. I suppose it's difficult keeping up a regular correspondence when you're always travelling."

"I suppose so," Drew remarked drily, a rigid look on his face.

"What is the matter with you?" Maggie demanded starting to lose patience with him. "You're behaving in an extraordinary manner. Your wife's in Moscow and you're not going to see her dance. You could at least find out which hotel she's . . . "

" . . . staying at and have a nice cosy romantic evening," he finished the sentence for her, irony heavy in his voice.

"Stop it, Drew," Maggie said quietly. It was getting nasty. "I'll see you some other time when you're in a better mood." She made an effort to go but Drew placed a restraining hand on her arm.

"I want to divorce Irina."

"Divorce!" Maggie repeated sitting

down. The word didn't make sense. "But — but I thought you were so happy."

"That's what everyone thought," he replied dismally. "But in here," and he patted the wallet in his inner pocket, "I have the evidence of her treachery."

"Irina has someone else? I don't understand."

Drew gave a sad smile.

"Our relationship had been unsatisfactory for a long time. Part of the trouble I suppose stemmed from the fact that we saw so little of each other. She was either away on tour or I was abroad on a business trip. Do you mind if I smoke?"

"Not at all."

He lit a slim cigar, took a puff and watched the blue smoke rise before continuing. "A few months ago Irina had a short break between engagements so I suggested we went away on a holiday together. I felt concerned; it was so obvious we were drifting apart.

"We set off on a tour of Scotland. It

was disastrous. Everything went wrong from the beginning, we could agree on nothing. One night our quarrelling reached a crisis. I said some vile things to her. Next morning she returned to London by train and I came back in the car.

"When I got back to Kingsley Magna I phoned her flat several times — she had a flat near the theatre — but there was always no reply. I phoned the theatre and left messages, they were always ignored. Then one night I was searching for something in our bedroom — can't remember what it was, something the accountant wanted, and in the waste paper basket I found an incriminating hotel receipt. Meesy had been in bed with flu so jobs like emptying waste paper baskets hadn't been done."

A look of pain seared Drew's face. "I couldn't believe it! Irina had a lover! I didn't know the name, it was no one in the company, and the date on the receipt was July. Last July she said she had strained her leg and had to stay in London for special physiotherapy treatment. The lying bitch! Well, the husband's always the last to know," he added bitterly.

"I went up to London the next day to confront her with it and demand a divorce. So many things now fitted into place — unexplained absences, her irritability towards me. At the theatre they told me the company had just left for a season in Moscow on the first leg of a world tour, so when I heard Joel was going to Moscow I decided to join the party."

Drew put his hand on the table and slowly clenched it. "My anger and frustration was such I couldn't wait until she returned." Maggie gave a shudder.

"The point is," he continued. "Will you help me?"

She looked into Drew's dark troubled eyes, startled at this request. "But how can I help?"

"I said some terrible things to her

in Scotland," Drew replied. "I'm sorry about it now but she drove me to it. Anyway, I'm pretty certain that if I present myself at the stagedoor tomorrow night there is a distinct possibility she will refuse to see me. She always liked you Maggie. She'd talk to you and all you have to do is go round to the stagedoor in the interval tomorrow night. Ask to see her then arrange to meet for say afternoon tea at the National Hotel the following afternoon, assuming of course she hasn't got a matinée."

"And you'll be there and take over?"

"Precisely," he replied tersely.

Maggie looked away, hesitating, not certain what to do. Not exactly a pleasant task being the go-between in a pending divorce case. Particularly when Irina was involved. She had seen her explosive temper in action on previous occasions. She was definitely not keen.

"Do it for me, Maggie," Drew urged. She turned and looked at him and his dark eyes stared into hers, pleading, begging. "I'm at the end of my rope," he added in an almost inaudible voice.

There had been a time when she had worshipped Drew, she thought. She would have done anything for him. It was only in adulthood that things had gone wrong, their relationship had soured. And suddenly it didn't matter and she felt a tremendous surge of pity for him.

"I'll do it," she said firmly. "I'll probably regret it, but I'll do it."

"You won't regret it, Maggie," and his face relaxed into a smile for the first time that evening.

The waitress was switching off the lights. It was time to go. They stood up and moved towards the door.

"Oh by the way," said Drew slowly. "This matter is private. If it ever got back to Dad, I don't think he could stand it right now — he's still very weak."

"I won't breathe a word to a soul."

"Thanks. Meet you here tomorrow night."

Drew opened the door and they walked out into the corridor.

"Got your wedding date fixed?" There was a hint of sarcasm in his voice.

"Not yet," Maggie replied evenly.

They had now reached the lift. "If you do marry Joel, it will be the worst thing you will ever do."

"Why ever should it be?" she demanded hotly. "Joel is the sweetest, kindest . . . "

"You'd be bored in a month," he said grinning at her. "Where are you going tomorrow?"

"The Metro."

"Don't get lost. Good night, Maggie and thanks again."

Maggie went alone up to the nineteenth floor.

★ ★ ★

The Metro proved to be unforgettable. They followed Greisha down a long escalator to the station platform. It was like walking into a stately home. There were crystal chandeliers, life-size statues in bronze reclining in alcoves, marble pillars and intricately carved white walls. A train rattled in and the illusion had gone.

Maggie, Bebe and Joel with the rest of the party boarded the train, the doors closed, and the train moved slowly out of the station. Maggie was strap hanging between Joel and Bebe.

"What's the matter, Joel," she asked. "You look so miserable."

"I don't want to talk about it," he replied in a depressed voice.

"But you must," she insisted. "If we have any misunderstandings we must put them right."

"I'll say," he replied with feeling. "Well it's about last night."

"You mean the circus?"

"I'm not talking about the circus. Last night I phoned your room half an hour after we said goodnight. You weren't there, because I kept it ringing so long . . ."

Maggie's face relaxed into a smile of relief. "For a minute I thought it was something serious. I was talking to Drew in the Tea Room. They make a very nice lemon tea."

"Why the sudden interest in drinking lemon tea with Drew?" he asked suspiciously. "I always thought I could trust you, Maggie."

They stood glaring at each other. The train stopped, the doors opened.

"Hey you two," called Mr Collins. "We've got to get off here."

They stepped into a station of stainless steel and mosaics of Ukrainian peasants.

"I want to know what you and Drew were up to last night."

"We weren't up to anything," replied Maggie trying to be patient. "We were just talking. The Tea Room's on the tenth floor and quite delightful. I recommend it."

"You just happened to be there and Drew walked in."

"No, Drew phoned my room and

asked me to meet him there. He just wanted to have a chat."

"He had all the time in the world to do that at the Karbatuk Restaurant . . . "

Greisha's voice took over:

" . . . the Soviet Union's finest architects, sculptors and artists built our metro system. Each station has its own unique design. The ventilation system changes the air eight times each hour. I will now take you to a station designed by Alexei Shchusev, the architect of Lenin's Mausoleum and the most celebrated architect of his day . . . "

"I'm just asking you to be honest with me, Maggie," Joel's voice pleaded as a train came in and they stepped aboard.

It was very crowded and Maggie found herself pushed next to Mr Collins, a librarian from Brixton and a young woman she hadn't spoken to before. The young woman came from Cumbria and their conversation absorbed her for the next few stops.

It was when she was going up an escalator with the rest of the party that Maggie realised Joel and Bebe were not in sight. Perhaps they were just ahead of her. It was more likely they had taken the wrong direction when they had alighted from the train. Her suspicions were confirmed when she boarded the waiting Intourist bus outside the station. Joel and Bebe were lost in the Moscow Metro system.

"It happens all the time," said Greisha with a nonchalant shrug of her shoulders.

There was no real problem thought Maggie as she waited for them in the hotel foyer. Joel had an excellent knowledge of Russian, he'd find his way back. But as the hours passed she grew more and more uneasy, glancing at her watch every quarter of an hour, passing the time writing postcards, and all the time tension mounting within her.

When at last they did arrive she was not in a happy mood and could not share Bebe's enthusiasm about the adventure. There was also something different about them — a quiet aura of contentment shone from both their eyes as if the experience had strengthened a bond between them.

"We got off at the wrong stop," Joel explained. "Stupid thing to do. I think it was because we got talking to a student. Anyway turned out to be a good thing because he's at Moscow University. I told him we have to spend a year at a Russian college so he kindly showed us round. I've gone right off it."

"What's the matter with the place?"

Joel pulled a face. "It's like a factory. I hope you weren't worried about us," he added casually. "There was no need."

"No," replied Maggie making an effort to keep calm. "I wasn't worried in the least."

Mr Collins approached. "Glad to see you back. We've been very worried about you, haven't we, Maggie. Now don't forget — it's an early start for the ballet tonight. Anyone late won't be allowed in until the first interval."

"I'd better go and change," said Maggie. "See you soon."

She dressed with extra care, as if putting on her best dress would make her feel better about it, the interview with Irina, the ordeal of having to ask her to meet for afternoon tea. Would she see through it, would she challenge her? She didn't know the answer. She only knew she had agreed to do it. She selected a black taffeta dress with a full skirt, a scolloped hemline and a deeply scooped out neckline. Then gathering her hair up she pushed it into a glittering chignon. A double row of pearls completed the outfit. She had worn the dress in the last play at Lazonby and the wardrobe mistress had allowed her to buy it.

It was almost time for the bus to leave and the first person Maggie saw in the foyer was Joel. He had made an effort and put on a dark suit and at the sight of her raised his eyebrows in admiration.

"You look stunning, Maggie." His eyes had a warm loving look in them. "I'd get lost with you any time."

Just then Mr Collins and Bebe walked across and joined them.

"It's not the Bolshoi," Mr Collins was saying.

"But it's got to be," Bebe replied. "In Moscow it's the Bolshoi."

"Mr Collins is right," smiled Maggie. "It's the Royal Westminster we're going to see tonight — they're on a cultural exchange."

"You mean the company Drew's wife is in," exclaimed Bebe. "Gee, what a thrill."

"Most unfortunate Drew has a prior engagement," said Mr Collins, "but fortunate for me."

"Prior engagement my foot," exclaimed Joel angrily. "He's being very unkind to Irina. I suppose they've had another of their tiffs."

"Or perhaps he's seen the ballets so

many times he's bored with them," suggested Bebe as they moved towards the hotel entrance. Joel gave her a derisory look.

It was a small nineteenth-century theatre with a five tiered crimson and gold auditorium. Stupendous crystal chandeliers hung from the high ceiling. Maggie sat between Joel and Bebe. What an invidious position Drew had placed her in. Joel had asked her to be honest with him and Drew had demanded secrecy. The lights dimmed and the curtain rose on 'Les Sylphides' and as Maggie watched the fluid movements of the dancers with their dark hair parted in the centre and demure downcast expressions, she searched for Irina in vain.

They all looked alike. She couldn't even pick out Julie Harris. The programme they had bought was of little use, it only gave the synopsis of the ballets.

"Can you see Irina?" she whispered to Joel who was scanning the stage with the binoculars he had hired from the cloakroom attendant.

He shook his head. "She must be in the ballet after the interval," he whispered back.

When the ballet came to an end and the lights came on Mr Collins suggested a cup of coffee in the refreshment room. As they sauntered up the crowded auditorium aisle Bebe turned to Maggie, her eyes shining.

"Gee, wasn't that just wonderful," she exclaimed excitedly. "I love the ballet. Do you think there is any chance of meeting her — Drew's wife."

"We'll go backstage after the show and invite her to our hotel," suggested Joel. "And any stupid row my brother's had with Irina they can damn well make it up."

They had now reached the corridor which led to the refreshment room. How could she disappear for five or ten minutes without arousing suspicion?

"Will you excuse me," she said turning to Joel quickly. "I — I just

113

want to powder my nose."

"I'll order you a coffee," Joel called as she disappeared into the milling crowd and made her way into the theatre foyer. Here she collected her coat and hurried out into the icy atmosphere wondering why she had agreed to such a foolhardy errand. Irina could be very difficult. Still, she only had to ask her to meet for afternoon tea, so what was she worrying about?

It was warm and cosy inside the stagedoor. An elderly man stood behind a counter and behind him letters for the company had been pushed into a slotted board. On another board were company announcements. The stagedoor keeper peered at her through thick lens glasses.

"I would like to see Irina Doestraskaya."

The old man shook his head and muttered something in Russian. Maggie looked round helplessly. Then a swing door down the passage opened and a fair-haired young man emerged and walked up to her.

"You look English," he said with a smile, "and in trouble."

"I am. I want to see Irina Doestraskaya."

"Don't we all." The fair-haired man replied with a weary note in his voice. "I'm Gavin Denby by the way, Assistant Stage Manager and general dog's body. The company has moved on to Leningrad and I've been left behind to clear up all the odds and ends."

Maggie gazed at him in astonishment. "Which ballet company are we seeing tonight?" she asked bewilderedly.

"It's the senior members of the Bolshoi Ballet School. The Royal Westminister moved on to Leningrad two days ago. Irina by the way isn't with the company." His voice again took on a weary tone. "But there is every chance she will turn up in Leningrad. To say Irina is unpredictable is putting it mildly, and the only reason we put up with her extraordinary behaviour is because she is one of the finest dancers

115

in the company. Are you going to Leningrad?"

"Yes, I believe we are."

"Look us up there — the Pavlovsk Theatre."

"Thanks, I'll do that."

Back in the theatre foyer Maggie handed her coat to the attendant, and hurried into the auditorium just as the lights were dimming.

"Where've you been?" Joel whispered, as she sat down. "I've been looking for you everywhere."

"Sorry Joel," she whispered back. "I met someone from England."

The curtain rose. How she hated lying to Joel, and all because of Drew. Why couldn't he sort out his own problems without dragging her into it.

"Irina isn't in this one," whispered Joel, as the dancers pirouetted about the stage.

"It isn't the Royal Westminster," Maggie whispered.

The ballet finally came to an end and after the principal dancers had taken their bows, received numerous bouquets thrown onto the stage from the admiring audience, Maggie, Joel and Bebe with Mr Collins left the theatre and returned to the hotel.

"It wasn't even her company," said Bebe pouting. "I feel so disappointed."

"Come and have a drink," suggested Joel.

They made their way down a wide staircase into a dimly lit room where the decor and furnishings appeared to be purple and silver. Taped music was playing Russian folk dances. It was 10.45. Drew would be waiting. At the bar was the girl from Cumbria and the librarian from Brixton. Mr Collins bought a round of drinks and the general conversation turned into a discussion as to whether or not there was still time to go dancing in the pavilion in Gorki Park.

"I feel too tired anyway," said Maggie. "You go with Bebe," she suggested looking at Joel.

And before Joel had time to start

arguing Maggie slipped away, up the staircase, then up in the lift to the tenth floor. Drew was waiting for her at the table nearest the door. She took off her coat, placing it over the bench and sat down. Drew looked at her admiringly.

"I must say your taste has improved. I remember another black dress . . . "

"I'd rather not remember it."

"Like some tea." He motioned the waitress to bring another cup. "Well, what did she say?" he asked, his fingers drumming on the pine table top.

"The company's moved on to Leningrad, and she's not with them."

"What do you mean she's not with them?" Drew demanded angrily.

"What I said — she's not with the company, but there is every possibility she will turn up in Leningrad. I gather she has done this sort of thing before — Gavin Denby said she's unpredictable."

"That's a nice way of saying she's damn unreliable. Well, I can vouch for that."

The waitress brought the cup and Maggie poured the tea.

"Like another one, Drew?"

"No thanks."

There was a small tremor in his right hand and in an effort to still it he clasped his hands together.

Poor Drew, Maggie thought compassionately. How he is suffering.

"I think everything's going to be all right," she said trying to reassure him.

He caught her hand and held it. "Glad you're so confident."

The sound of the door opening made her look. To her dismay Joel was standing there with such a sad look of accusation in his eyes.

"You're a cheat Maggie."

6

TEARS sprang to Maggie's eyes as Joel gave her a withering look and closed the door. She spun round to Drew her cheeks flushed with anger.

"Now look what you've done," she stormed. "You've damaged my relationship with Joel. Can't you solve your own problems without dragging me into it?"

"Calm down, Maggie." Drew's matter-of-fact voice only infuriated her more.

"Can't you see you're ruining my life?"

"Don't talk nonsense," he retorted sharply. "First you didn't have to go to the stagedoor. I didn't browbeat you into it."

"You were almost on your knees."

"And as for damaging your relationship with my brother," he continued smoothly, "I don't think you had much of one to begin with."

"You seem to have forgotten Joel has asked me to marry him," she informed him in a cold voice giving him a disdainful look.

"I haven't forgotten. He also proposed to a girl when he was taking his English degree."

"What happened years ago has nothing to do with the present — Joel and I love each other, a subject on which you know very little."

"I could say the same for you," he hit back. "Have you slept with him?"

"Of course not."

"Then you don't know him. Why don't you grow up, Maggie? I should have thought being an actress would have given you a bit more maturity."

"I don't sleep around, if that's what you're getting at."

"Platonic friendships at your Lazonby Theatre?" Drew enquired a mischievous smile on his face.

"On my part — yes. I'm very choosy.

Why don't you try to be nice to me for a change?"

"I'm willing to do that anytime," he said stroking his fingers around the palm of her hand.

"Don't." She snatched her hand away, as if his touch scalded.

"We are on edge tonight. What's the matter, Maggie?"

"It wasn't such a good idea coming on this trip." Maggie stood up and slipped her coat over her shoulders.

"What makes you say that?" Drew asked, an amused look on his face.

"It's not what I thought it was going to be."

"Expectations too high," he replied sourly. "We are all guilty of it." They moved towards the door. "Am I right in thinking we take the train to Leningrad tomorrow?"

Maggie nodded. "Leaves at twelve noon, and this time you go to the stagedoor. I've had enough. It's the Pavlosk Theatre by the way."

Drew smiled at her. "Don't worry,

Maggie. I've got the message. From now on I'm on my own."

Drew held the door open for her and they walked out into the corridor. There was a downcast expression on Drew's face.

"Look Drew, I'm really sorry about the trouble you're having with Irina, but it upset me tonight having to lie to Joel. I told him I was too tired to go dancing in order to get to the Tea Room, and at the theatre, heavens knows what he thought when I disappeared for so long."

Drew gave her a sympathetic look. "I appreciate what you did tonight even though nothing's come of it. I think the trouble with me is I'm being overprotective towards Dad. Look, I'll tell Joel all about it at the first opportunity. That satisfy you?"

Maggie smiled happily. "Thanks, Drew."

They parted at the lifts. Drew wanted to go out for a brief walk along Gorki Street before retiring to bed so Maggie took the lift up to the nineteenth floor alone. She walked slowly down the oak-panelled corridor, and as she passed Joel's door on a sudden impulse decided to knock. She must talk to him — allay his fears.

Joel did not open the door so Maggie knocked again and waited. He must have gone to the bar for solace she thought feeling disappointed. She continued down the corridor and let herself into her room. She would just have to wait until morning. Drew would probably speak to him anyway at breakfast, if not there would be an opportunity on the train. He'd understand and everything would be as before.

She got into bed and switched off the bedside lamp. It was the first serious misunderstanding she had had with Joel and it disturbed her. All because of Drew. If only she hadn't agreed to be his messenger girl none of this would have happened.

It was still dark when she awoke.

She was cold and getting out of bed touched the radiator. Not surprisingly it was cold. She would report it to Greisha in the morning and in the meantime what she needed was an extra blanket. She glanced at her wrist watch; it was half-past three.

After a fruitless search in all the cupboards and drawers, Maggie slipped on her dressing-gown, took her phrase book out of her handbag and finally found the Russian word for 'blanket'.

The floor lady sat behind her desk, her grey head nodding on her chest.

"*Izvinitye*," said Maggie softly as she approached.

At the sound of her voice the woman opened her eyes with a start.

"*Adiyala*," said Maggie slowly.

The floor lady's face was a blank and she muttered something in Russian. Mime it thought Maggie desperately, so folding her arms together she made a pretence of shivering. Instantly the woman's face lit up with recognition.

"*Adiyala!*" she exclaimed delighted

she had understood.

Disappearing into a nearby room she returned a few moments later carrying a blanket.

"*Spasiba*," said Maggie gratefully and taking the blanket from her started the walk down the long straight corridor. Suddenly she stopped, frozen to the spot. Joel came out of a room on the right, hurried across the corridor, and then entered his room on the left. His whole manner suggested stealth, furtiveness. He was like a thief in the night.

She continued down the corridor and when she drew level with Joel's room she paused. The room directly across the corridor was Bebe's. Joel of all people, so straight-laced and puritanical. It was unbelievable.

When she reached her room she collapsed into an armchair stunned and dazed. Now she knew the reason why she had not been able to get an answer when she had knocked at Joel's door earlier in the evening. After their unfortunate encounter in the Tea Room he had gone straight to Bebe's room for a different kind of consolation. And Bebe alone and unhappy on the rebound from Guy would have been only too pleased to give it.

She spread the blanket on the bed and climbed in. What happens now she thought miserably staring into the dark. She had never felt so alone; her world seemed to be crumbling about her. In the cold light of day she told herself, when Joel has explained his conduct, this situation will dissolve into trivia. This thought comforted her and she fell asleep.

She awoke late. First she couldn't find her hairbrush; then one of her earrings was missing and by the time she got in the dining-room only a few latecomers were still taking breakfast. One of them was the girl from Cumbria.

"Fashion here is twenty years out of date," she announced, "but I just love those silver fox hats. They're absolutely timeless. I must buy one before I leave.

Why don't you, Maggie? You'd look stunning in one."

"Actually I've decided to buy one," Maggie replied. It was more pleasant to think of hats than Joel and Bebe. "We don't have much time left in Moscow so it will have to be Leningrad. Have you packed by the way?"

"Did it last night," replied the girl. "I learnt from hard experience on the southern Russian tour last year. Did you know we arrived in Samarkand . . . "

Maggie drained her coffee cup. "If you will excuse me." She hadn't packed a thing and the luggage had to be in the foyer in thirty minutes.

Up in her room as she flung her few belongings into the case and zipped it up she had a sudden dread of the day and an unreasonable longing to remain in Moscow. But it wasn't a practical idea, there would be too many problems changing the air tickets and Greisha would probably say it was impossible anyway.

At the lift she met Bebe wearing a hip-length fur jacket that looked suspiciously like mink.

"You should have come last night Maggie," Bebe smiled pleasantly. "It was incredible. A sort of nineteen-thirties time lock, Russian style."

"I wish I had," said Maggie. It was taking all her self-control to speak in a civil manner. "What time did you get back?"

"Around midnight I guess. It wasn't really our scene. Then Joel took me out again — the National Bar just five minutes round the corner. He said you were too busy to come. We had a great time. Gee, all the action's there!" She put her hand over her mouth stifling a yawn. "I'm so tired. Must have been half past three when we got back from there."

"Half-past three!" Maggie could have hugged her. They stepped into the lift and glided noiselessly down to the ground floor. That was the time she was on the corridor. How could

129

she have misjudged them. She felt ashamed.

"I'm glad you had a good time," she said with full sincerity.

In the foyer Bebe dashed off to change some travellers' cheques. Maggie found Joel by the newspaper stand reading a copy of *Pravda.*

"Joel," she said with a sheepish look on her face. "I want to explain about last night. You see Drew wants a divorce . . . "

"It's all right, sweetie," he cut in smiling happily. "He's told me all about it."

"I'm so relieved. The whole thing was so stupid. I wish now I'd gone with you. I understand you stayed late at the National Bar."

"Too true. Spent a fortune on drinks. Still it's holiday time." Joel's eyes were searching the crowded hotel foyer. He's looking for Bebe, thought Maggie suddenly, and the contentment she had experienced in the last few minutes vanished.

"You don't trust me," she said accusingly at Joel.

"Of course I trust you." Joel's eyes came back at her. His smile seemed patronising.

"You didn't last night."

He put his hand into hers and kissed her cheek lightly.

"Come now, Maggie. No more quarrelling."

"Sorry, Joel. I'm being a bit unreasonable today."

The train for Leningrad moved slowly out of the Moscow station. Maggie was seated next to Mr Collins and Joel and Drew were directly across the aisle. She couldn't see Bebe. Maggie glanced curiously around her. The interior of the coach was shabby, made one think of the 1920s, and at the windows hung faded green cotton curtains with another piece of white fabric stretched across the lower half making the viewing area very small indeed.

They were travelling through the

suburbs of Moscow, mile upon mile of cream-coloured tower blocks of workers' flats. After a while she grew tired of this monotonous scenery and turned to Joel. He handed her his copy of *Pravda*. It was an English version. She opened it and read about the factory that had produced more than its planned level and the worker who had received the Order of the Red Banner of Labour. She was just reading about the good harvest expected in the south when Mr Collins turned to her.

"Don't believe a word of it," he said offering Maggie a caramel from a large white paper bag.

"The expected good harvest. They've never had a good one yet. And as for the factory that produced more than the planned level, it's just not true. You must forgive me but I spent most of my life teaching Russian history. I was at the Henry the Eighth at Littlebourne. Do you know it?"

"I'm afraid I don't."

Mr Collins looked disappointed.

"Strange isn't it, I spent my life complaining about the young blighters, now I miss them." He placed his hand on his forehead and frowned.

"Got a headache?" asked Maggie sympathetically.

Mr Collins nodded. "Went to the National Bar last night. Sort of place where everyone goes sooner or later — international journalists, black marketeers."

"You must have seen Joel and Bebe," said Maggie looking interested.

"Can't say I did," said Mr Collins thoughtfully.

"You must have," insisted Maggie. "They definitely went there last night."

"Of course I remember now. Bebe's the American girl. Yes, they popped in just after midnight. They only stayed about ten minutes. Can't blame them. The drinks were terribly expensive."

"Where did they go to — another bar?" asked Maggie hopefully.

"Oh no, they went back to the hotel. The American girl said she wanted to

133

go to bed — it had been a long day."

"Yes of course."

It was an odd sort of feeling. Maggie felt neither anger nor sorrow. In fact emotionally she felt dead. It must be like this she thought when people are in a state of shock. The reaction comes later.

She gave Joel his paper back without even looking at him, then got up and went into the next coach where she found an uncluttered window on a corridor. She had to be alone if only for a few minutes. They were now travelling through silver birch forests and lakes. She stood at the window a long time. She felt quite calm. Her mind seemed to have blotted out Joel. After a while the forest made her think of Russian fairy-tales. That made her think of the ballet, Irina and finally Drew. Could she never escape these Brooksby men? Would her mind always go round in circles? Perhaps when Dad solved his financial problems she should emigrate to Australia? European actresses usually did well down under. It was worth thinking about.

This thought cheered her up so much she returned to her seat. Joel's seat was empty but Drew looked up from his book and gave her an enquiring look.

"I thought you'd decided to jump train," he said closing his book as she sat down. "Like to come to the dining-car for a spot of refreshment?

"Not a bad idea. Where's Joel?"

"Not a clue."

It was quite a walk to the dining-car. A lot of military were travelling and some coaches had their own coach lady to attend to their wants.

In the dining-car the white cloths were stained and the flowers were plastic, still, the bowls of hot soup were tasty, and the slices of sweet dark brown bread nourishing. They ate in silence. Then Drew ordered coffee and turned to Maggie with an enquiring look.

"You're too quiet Maggie, not like you at all. If you're worrying about

Joel, forget it. I've told him all my troubles, and we've agreed I was being overprotective towards Dad. There's going to be a divorce and he's going to learn about it sooner or later. Also I suffer from too much pride." He gave her a crest-fallen look.

"I understand."

A stout woman in overalls placed the coffee before them. Maggie knew how much Drew hated failure. She put a spoonful of sugar in her cup.

"It's something else, isn't it?" he persisted. "You look as though the end of the world is near."

Suddenly Maggie's eyes pricked with tears. "Do you think there's any chance of catching an earlier plane home?"

"Might be possible. You'd have to see Greisha. But I warn you the Russians don't like people upsetting their schedules." Drew gave her a thoughtful look. "Can't you tell me what it is?"

"I just want to go home," she said stubbornly.

They drank their coffee in silence for a few minutes and then Drew said:

"I'll be glad to get back too."

"After you've seen Irina?"

"After I've seen Irina." He tightened his lips as if an irritating thought had occurred to him and then decided not to discuss it.

"Still interested in the night sky?" he asked suddenly.

Maggie smiled. "I'm amazed you remembered. Yes I'm still interested. After an evening performance at the theatre it used to take me ages to relax, so I used to let the adrenalin disperse by sitting in the window seat in my room star-gazing."

"Sounds delightful."

"Did you see Mars in September?"

"No. I'm not awake at three o'clock in the morning."

"It was incredible. It really is the red planet. You miss such a lot by sleeping."

"Sleeping is an unfortunate habit I have like eating. Irina was like you,

137

when she returned from an evening performance she couldn't relax until the small hours. Very trying for the partner who's on a different work schedule."

"So there were periods when you actually lived together."

"Short, I must admit and trying."

"I suppose you're filled with bitterness and regret."

"I've got over that now," said Drew with a smile. "It was an experience I had to go through to learn. I should have realised that such a passionate woman as Irina, away for months at a time, would be bound to take a lover. She wouldn't be able to help herself. She wouldn't be able to keep her passions under control. I am an artiste she used to say. I must not be inhibited. My God, what a fool I was listening to all that crap."

Drew clenched his fists and banged the table. "Let's go back to the coach."

When they returned to their seats Joel was there reading *War and Peace*.

"The journey's not that long," Drew

commented with an amused look on his face. Joel stood up to let him sit down. "What was the food like — someone saw you in the dining-car."

"Not recommended but it passes the time."

Maggie took her seat next to Mr Collins and Joel returned to his book. There was such a placid, innocent expression on his face it angered Maggie. He was the cheat, not her! She sat smouldering for a while. At length she could stand it no longer.

"Where's Bebe?" she demanded.

Joel looked up over the top of his book. "She went into the next coach." Then his eyes went back to the page.

"How many more hours have we got on this train?"

Joel looked up again from his book. "Five. We've just past Glinyna. Look Maggie do you mind if I finish this chapter?"

"Yes I do mind." Then she lowered her voice and leaned across the aisle. "I know exactly what happened last night. You and Bebe have lied to me. How could you do it?"

Joel's face was a picture of misunderstood innocence. "Do what? I don't comprehend."

"You comprehend all right. I saw you leave Bebe's room around three-thirty this morning."

Joel closed his book. "Have a bit of compassion, Maggie. Don't you know what it's like to be jilted. Bebe hasn't got over it. When we're all together she puts on a brave face but underneath she's breaking her heart. Last night when I took her back to her room from the National Bar she became so distressed I couldn't leave her. I was afraid she might throw herself out of the window or take an overdose. Try to have a bit of understanding, Maggie."

Joel looked at her beseechingly, his usual tranquil eyes dull with anxiety, and Maggie in return looked highly embarrassed.

"I'm sorry, Joel." She spoke in a

140

subdued voice and Joel leaned across the aisle and patted her hand.

"Don't think anymore about it. You just read the signals wrong."

"Hi!" said an American voice and Maggie looked up to see Bebe standing before them, her fur jacket draped nonchalantly over her shoulders, her long blonde hair hiding part of her face.

"Made new friends?" Maggie asked hopefully.

"I'll say!" Her eyes were shining. "Americans. It's great talking to them. One of them's from Long Island!"

"You'll have a lot to talk about. Meeting up again in Leningrad?"

"Probably I guess." Then Bebe turned her attention to Joel. "Like to come back with me and I'll introduce you. You too, Maggie," she added as an afterthought. "One of them's a journalist and just come back from Siberia."

Joel stood up and as he gazed at Bebe there was an unmistakable look of warmth in his eyes. Then suddenly as if remembering Maggie was there he turned to her.

"Like to come too, Maggie?"

"I might join you later."

As she watched Joel follow Bebe down the swaying coach she had the curious feeling she was merely an onlooker, a third party, and that as the days went by Bebe appeared to be gaining in importance in Joel's life. Yet it was she who was engaged to him. What had made him propose in the first place? Childhood memories? Was it a strong enough basis on which to build a marriage. Or was it that Drew's doubts about the relationship were beginning to influence her? Mr Collins touched her arm.

"Haven't been in Leningrad for twenty years," he said nostalgically. "Well, that's where it all happened."

"What happened?" asked Maggie, her mind still on Joel.

"The nineteen-seventeen," he replied patiently.

"Of course. Silly of me."

"The night it happened the trams were running, people were going out to dinner, the theatres were crowded, Chaliapin was singing at the opera. Most people didn't know a revolution was taking place."

"How incredible!" exclaimed Maggie.

"The Red Guards first took over the post office and other principal buildings," continued Mr Collins, "then finally they entered the Winter Palace at two-twenty-five am. Antonov, a member of the Military Revolutionary Committee entered the room where the provisional government was still sitting and shouted, 'In the name of the Military Revolutionary Committee I declare you all under arrest.' And that was the end of old Russia. I hope I'm not boring you?"

"No of course not. Please continue."

Talk for as long as you want Mr Collins thought Maggie. Anything to stop me thinking of Joel and Bebe. Half an hour later when Mr Collins decided that Maggie's history lesson had finished for the day she looked across the aisle. Joel's seat was still empty and Drew was asleep, and in his sleep the stress lines had gone from his face. He looked a younger, carefree Drew, like the man she used to know. Suddenly he stirred and opened his eyes.

"Why didn't we fly to Leningrad," he grumbled. "I hate train journeys. Like to have a coffee?"

It had now gone dark. They started the journey to the dining-car, the train rumbling through a town but all that could be seen was the twinkling lights in the darkness. Drew sat opposite Maggie and ordered the coffee, and the lonely, troubled look returned as he scrutinised her face.

"You've changed a lot, Maggie."

"For the better I hope."

"Of course. Your life in Cumbria obviously suits you."

"I've lost my job remember?"

"A girl with your looks and ability

can do anything."

She gave him a hard look. "You've changed, Drew. I don't normally get compliments from you. Or are you up to something devious?"

"Why are you always on the defensive?"

"I have to be."

"Not with me."

"With you more than anyone."

Drew gave her a patronising smile. "Relax, Maggie; you're like a time bomb."

"It's all very well for you," she retorted. "Everything just falls into your lap."

"It doesn't." He gave her a hard look, his mouth tense.

"Sorry, Drew. I was thinking of your financial position."

From his pocket he brought out a packet of cigarettes and lit one.

"Like one?"

"No thanks. You know I don't smoke, and neither did you."

"I know but it helps."

She watched him draw on the cigarette feeling his inner tension.

"Yes, when Dad dies I'll inherit Kingsley Magna," he said in a flat voice, "and there's a rumour I may be offered a directorship at International . . ." he stopped.

"You'll feel better when you've seen Irina."

"I want that divorce and quick," he said grimly. "Like another coffee?"

"No thanks."

He talked for a while about his job whilst Maggie listened interested. Then he stubbed out his cigarette.

"Like to go back to the coach?"

Maggie picked up her bag and they turned to go. It was then that she saw Joel at the end of the dining-car deep in conversation with a man. He was stoutish wearing a brown leather coat.

7

MAGGIE followed Drew along the swaying corridor, thinking about the man in the brown leather coat. She had seen him somewhere before. It wasn't the Moscow hotel, nor the circus or ballet. It was when they reached their coach she remembered. He was the man she had seen Drew talking to in the Moscow street the day she had gone alone with Joel to the Kremlin.

"Your Moscow friend is on the train," she told Drew as they sat down. "Joel's talking to him in the dining-car. I noticed him just as we were leaving but couldn't remember who he was until now."

Drew looked puzzled for a moment until he remembered.

"You mean Nikolai! He didn't say a word about going to Leningrad. Must be something that suddenly cropped up. What's the matter, Maggie. You look tensed up about something?"

Maggie gave an embarrassed laugh. "I know it sounds silly, but there's something about him I don't like, something shifty."

"Nikolai is one of the nicest people you could ever meet," replied Drew indignantly. "I shall go to the dining-car, bring him back and introduce you to him, then you will see how wrong you are."

Maggie took a slim volume out of her handbag. Drew was very fond of doing that, proving he was in the right. "When Joel realises Nikolai knows you he'll bring him back anyway," she said coldly opening her book.

There was a smile hovering about Drew's lips. "What are you reading?"

"*Springs of Chinese Wisdom*," Maggie replied without looking up.

"Sounds interesting. Read me something."

"'Demand much of yourself and

expect little from others. Thus you will be spared much vexation'," she read.

"If I were you I'd follow that."

"I certainly will. Here's another: 'Love is devotion without the slightest deliberation'."

She looked up and Drew's eyes held hers. "Do you believe that?" he asked softly.

"Yes," she replied without hesitation.

"You're very innocent."

"You're world-weary."

"And pure into the bargain." She must have touched a weak spot; ridicule had crept into his voice.

"If I had something heavy I'd throw it at you."

Drew threw back his head and laughed. "You haven't got red hair for nothing. How's your father getting along with his black-faced Suffolks?"

"Black-faced Swaledales if you don't mind. You wouldn't believe the things that can go wrong with sheep and the years we have late snowfalls are disastrous. Sometimes I catch him

149

looking at photos taken at Kingsley Magna. Remember when one of his charolais bulls won a prize?"

Drew nodded reminiscently. "Your father's a charolais man. Any chance of him coming back. We haven't anyone at the moment."

"I think he'd like to but he's a proud man and he's not going to admit he made a mistake. When he inherited the farm he should have sold it — there's little money in sheep, and I know his financial position is not healthy."

"Perhaps you'd have a word with him when you get back. How would you feel about moving back to Kingsley Magna?" Drew watched her reaction carefully.

"Kingsley Magna was my home for most of my life," she replied. "If you remember I was born there."

Drew laughed. "And as a small child used to wander off and get lost so that your distraught mother had to organise a search party to find you."

Maggie laughed softly recalling the

memory of her mother — a woman who had made the world seem so cosy and secure. Drew returned to his book and Maggie continued reading *Chinese Wisdom* but the mood had gone. What was going to happen to Dad? It made sense selling the farm and returning to the Brooksbys' as estate manager. She'd test his reaction when she got back.

The train was now passing through a built-up area with lights from tower blocks and factories blazing in the darkness. The army officer behind started taking his luggage off the overhead rack.

"I think we're approaching Leningrad," said Drew standing up. "I'm stiff. I feel I could go for a ten-mile hike. Do you do much climbing in Cumbria?"

"When I get a chance," Maggie smiled. Drew leaned forward taking his bag from the overhead rack, and Maggie stood up and put on her coat.

"I tried Roman Fell a few weeks ago

and forgot the light starts to fade early and had to turn back . . . "

She stopped. There was movement behind her and turning she saw Nikolai and Joel approaching down the centre aisle of the swaying coach.

"Brought you an old friend, Drew," smiled Joel. "Met Nikolai in the dining-car." He turned to Nikolai with a wave of his hand.

"Why didn't you tell me you were going to Leningrad?" demanded Drew putting his arm round Nikolai's shoulder.

"I did not know until this morning," replied Nikolai solemnly. "It is a coincidence I am speaking to your brother in the dining-car. I am drinking a quiet cup of coffee and the young man at the table starts speaking to me. He wishes to practise his Russian. Then I discover he is the brother of my friend."

Nikolai then turned to Maggie with an enquiring smile.

"May I introduce Maggie," said Drew. "She is Joel's fiancée."

Nikolai shook her hand. "Soon you will marry."

"The sooner the better," smiled Joel happily.

"We must meet in Leningrad," said Nikolai. "Are you going to the opera tomorrow night."

"Yes," replied Maggie. "We told our guide/interpreter we would like to go."

"Then I will see you there. We make a definite arrangement to meet after the performance."

The train now entered Leningrad station and came slowly to a halt. In the freezing darkness, pierced by a few overhead lamps, the passengers alighted from the train.

"What an extraordinary thing," exclaimed Maggie as she hurried along the platform with Joel, hard on the heels of Nikolai and Drew. "He's the man who was speaking to Drew when the bus stopped at the traffic lights — do you remember that day when we went to the Kremlin."

"Drew's pleased to see him again," Joel replied. "Nikolai's a nice chap. After the theatre he's going to take us to his brother's apartment. What's so extraordinary?"

"Hi!" Bebe appeared between them, her blue eyes sleepy, her head buried into her fur collar.

"Who's the Russian Drew's talking to?" she asked taking hold of both their arms.

"A guy I met in the dining-car," Joel explained. "We're meeting tomorrow night."

"Great!" she exclaimed with enthusiasm. "I love meeting Russians."

Maggie gave her a sideways stare.

In the station yard they boarded the waiting Intourist bus. Sleepy from the day's train journey, Leningrad was just a blur of crowded streets and bright lights. The hotel they had been allocated was modern; the ground floor boasting an indoor garden where tropical plants bloomed, birds sang and water fell into small pools.

Dinner had been arranged in a vast dining-room that had an almost theatrical atmosphere, with tables on varying levels leading down to a dance floor where a young man sat at a black grand piano playing preludes by Rachmaninoff. Maggie ate the caviar, the beef stroganoff, the ice cream, then as the meal came to an end, feeling an overwhelming desire for sleep she rose from the table, bid goodnight to everyone, and proceeded up the wide staircase.

As she passed the tropical garden Joel's voice called from behind.

"Hey, Maggie. What's the big hurry."

"I'm tired," she said, pressing the button for the lift.

"Me too," said Joel.

They went up in the crowded lift, then along the corridor to Maggie's room. When they reached her door Joel took the key from her, inserted it into the lock, and they both entered the wood-panelled room together.

"I don't like the way you've been

looking at me today," he said, his arms encircling her waist and drawing her close to him. "You've got to believe me about last night. I would never do anything to hurt you."

She looked up into his face, normally unburdened by care, now there were lines of strain about the mouth and his eyes had a weary look.

"Of course I believe you, Joel."

In return he kissed her forehead, the tip of her nose, then finally his mouth found hers. It was a gentle, tender, undemanding kiss.

"Everything's going to be all right, Maggie. It's just a question of faith and trust."

"I know," she murmured against his cheek.

"Like to go to the Winter Palace tomorrow?"

"Love to."

"I'll go and tell Greisha." He moved towards the door adding with a smile, "We don't have to go with her, but it's easier."

"Joel," said Maggie walking to the door a sudden earnest look on her face. "When you have your year in a Russian university, will Bebe go too?"

"Of course. She's on my course." Then an anxious look clouded his eyes. "You're being silly. No one could take your place."

She kissed his cheek. "See you at breakfast."

When Joel had gone Maggie decided to have a bath, and as she lay there in the scented water rubbing shampoo into her hair she suddenly realised there was an essential ingredient missing from her relationship with Joel. What it was she wasn't sure. She loved him, that was certain. She wanted to care for him, she was interested in his career; then she suddenly realised what it was. There was no excitement in the relationship. It will come later she thought. I must be patient.

Next morning when Maggie awoke she walked across to the window and drew back the vast curtains that covered the entire length of one wall to reveal an astonishing view of the River Neva. It was broad at that point, and on the far bank stood elegant eighteenth-century palaces with façades of Corinthian pillars and the exteriors painted white and gold. It made her think of a northern Canaletto, that is if you ignored the trams that rattled over the bridge at regular intervals, and the elderly woman in her dark coat and white head scarf sweeping the street below.

Overhead the dark sky threatened snow. She dressed in warm trousers, then unwrapped the copy of the *Cumbrian Times* that covered her boots. That was Dad's idea. When she was packing she had called down to him to see if she had left her boots in the hall and he had come up the stairs with them wrapped in the newspaper.

She was just about to throw it in the waste basket when her eye caught an advertisement. 'Hall to let in Windermere', she read. Windermere was always packed with visitors although the numbers did drop in the winter months. It could be a start for her own theatrical company. At Lazonby she had had a spell of stage managing, and once when the girl was ill had taken over in the box office. And what with playing everything from leads to walk-ons she felt reasonably confident.

She went down to the dining-room in good spirits. There might even be some of the Lazonby people interested in joining her. She was still in good spirits some two hours later standing in historic Palace Square in a freezing wind, with the Winter Palace on one side, and on the other a triumphant arch carrying a bronze chariot and horses.

"How the Russians love enormous squares," commented Joel looking around him. "You could get a battalion of tanks in here."

Bebe brought out her camera. "Let me take your picture."

Maggie stood between Drew and

Joel. They smiled and Bebe's camera clicked.

"What's your address in England, Maggie?" she asked looking around for another view. "We'll send you a copy."

The shadow came back; the feeling of being the third party. "Mirbeck Farm, Mirbeck," she murmured not caring whether she received a copy or not. 'We' — what the hell did she mean?

They joined the queue and entered the Winter Palace, standing in a white and gold room supported by green marble pillars. Greisha took over:

"This museum is composed of three buildings; the Winter Palace, the Small Hermitage and the Large Hermitage. The Small Hermitage was first used as a retreat for the Empress Catherine then later used for the Imperial Art collection . . . "

Drew was pushing his way through the crowd towards her.

"I'm thinking of going to the

Pavlovsk Theatre this afternoon," he whispered. "Like to come?"

"I thought we'd discussed this."

"I know, but I thought you'd like to see your friend Julie. You were great friends at one time."

"I'd like to see her," Maggie replied thoughtfully. "Ages since we met. Yes, I will come."

The party moved into the room of the twenty-five chandeliers. Joel was waiting for her at the door.

"Bebe suggests that this afternoon we break away from Greisha and go it alone round Leningrad. What do you say?"

"Sorry, Joel, but I've just told Drew I'll go with him to the Pavlovsk Theatre. You see I might have a chance of seeing . . ."

"Why on earth do you have to go with him?" Joel interrupted irritably.

"Give me a chance to finish. My old friend Julie Harris is with the company and it's an opportunity to meet and have a chat. Why don't you come too?"

"Julie and I never were exactly bosom pals. Anyway why have you suddenly become interested in her." He scowled at Maggie. "You haven't bothered to contact her before."

"I know. It was very remiss of me but I'd really like to see her again."

"Is it really Julie you want to see?" he asked suspiciously.

"What else could it be? Really Joel, you're being most unreasonable."

"I know," he replied miserably. "Where you're concerned I just can't help it."

He walked away from her as if the conversation was too painful to continue. In the next room a fountain played. Maggie stood there listening to the sound of flowing water. It was a soothing sound. There was no foundation for Joel's jealousy of Drew. All she had done was try to help Drew solve his matrimonial problems and not succeeded in the slightest. Mr Collins stood beside her.

"Exquisite, isn't it?" he murmured

stroking his beard. "Erected by a past emperor. The water in the fountain represents the tears he shed for a dead love."

Maggie turned away, a wave of emotion engulfing her. Drew was standing by a window, a solitary, lonely figure. She looked at his strong profile, his broad shoulders, his manliness. And she remembered a time when she had shed tears for him. It was so long ago it seemed it was another person who had shed those tears. Time heals as the emperor would have discovered, for today her feelings towards Drew were completely neutral.

In the afternoon she set off with Drew on foot to find the Pavlovsk Theatre. It had been an unpleasant lunch with Joel sulking so much she had very nearly cancelled her arrangements to go with Drew.

As they crossed the bridge it started to snow and the streets they walked along were shabby, the men and women who hurried past they too were shabby;

and haggard-looking women stood at the kerb selling apples and cabbages from broken metal containers. It was all very depressing. Then suddenly they turned into the Nevsky Prospekt. Here was a comparative prosperity, and the people who passed had a more purposeful air about them. They soon found the theatre with the aid of the map Drew had purchased at the hotel. Again the stagedoor keeper did not speak English. Suddenly the outer door opened and in rushed half a dozen young women. One of them was Julie.

"Maggie! Drew!" Julie exclaimed, her hazel eyes shining. "I can't believe it. Why didn't you let me know you were coming?" She was wearing a white woollen hat pulled down over her ears, her cheeks pink from the freezing atmosphere outside.

"Actually I didn't know your company was here until a few days ago," Maggie explained as she gave her a hug.

"If you're hoping to see Irina, I'm

afraid you're out of luck," said Julie turning to Drew. "She flew over with us then just disappeared. It's caused the most awful trouble. Ashley Morris — he's the director, he's hopping mad."

"What do you think could have happened?" Drew asked frowning heavily.

Julie shrugged her shoulders. "Like to see Ashley?"

"I certainly would."

"Follow me."

They followed Julie through the inner swing doors, then along a long stone-flagged corridor. Stagehands passed them, and in the distance could be heard the tinkling of a practice piano and the commands of the ballet mistress.

"Wonderful seeing you again, Maggie," said Julie turning round. "Engaged? Married?"

"Engaged to Joel."

"Congratulations. Don't forget to invite me to the wedding."

Julie had now stopped before a door at the end of the corridor.

"This is Ashley's room. Look, at four o'clock we get a half-hour break. What about a quick cup of tea at the Vaselevsky. You can't miss it in the Stapana Stijna."

She hurried off and Drew knocked at the door.

"Come in," called a distant masculine voice.

They walked into a small room, poorly lit by a little window and behind the desk sat a slim handsome man in his fifties. As they approached his desk he stood up and extended his hand.

"Drew Brooksby," said Drew shaking his hand.

"I remember you," said Ashley. "You're Irina's husband. Met you at one of the end-of-season dos." Then he turned and looked at Maggie quizzically.

"And this is a friend, Maggie Kerr."

Ashley Morris politely shook her hand.

"Do sit down. I gather you are here to see Irina. Well you're in for a disappointment. She's not with us and what she's up to God only knows." He sat down and rubbed his hand wearily across his forehead. "In fact I've been so worried I've decided to give her another twenty-four hours then I'm informing the British Embassy. And apart from that she has put me in a very difficult position. It just so happens we haven't got an understudy for her part in 'The Enchanted Horse', so if she doesn't turn up by Friday we will have to cancel the ballet. Can you help us Mr Brooksby? Do you have any idea where she might be?"

"I'm sorry, I can't help," confessed Drew. "The last time I saw her was when we were on holiday together in the early autumn."

Ashley Morris looked as though he didn't believe Drew.

"Any clue you could give us. Any lead?"

"I'm terribly sorry." Drew looked

167

embarrassed. "All I can think is she may be ill somewhere."

"Then why didn't she contact us, or get someone to do it on her behalf. She knows we must meet our contractual obligations. She must know the invidious position I'm in."

After that there seemed to be nothing more to say. Ashley Morris shook hands with them both and opened the door. The piano was still playing.

"I'll do my best to find her," said Drew.

"Thanks." Ashley Morris closed the door.

"What's that place Julie suggested?" asked Drew as they walked down the corridor.

"The Vaselevsky," said Maggie glumly. "Stapana Stijna."

The Vaselevsky was one of those Russian hotels straight out of the nineteenth century, cluttered with heavy mahogany furniture set amidst marble pillars. In the tea room the waitresses in black dresses and white caps and aprons, reminiscent of England in the 1930s flitted from table to table, whilst above the chandelier rose a vast empty space.

Tea was ordered. Drew sat opposite Maggie slumped in despondency.

"It's not as bad as it seems, Drew," said Maggie trying to think of something to console him. "If she has disappeared into thin air you'll just have to get a divorce on the grounds of desertion. I know it takes years, but there's no alternative."

"All very well for you to talk," he exploded. "So easy to give advice. Anyway you're the cause of the whole damn mess."

"Me!" she exclaimed in utter astonishment.

"Yes. You!"

8

MAGGIE gazed at Drew in utter stupefaction as the waitress brought the tea.

"I don't understand what you're talking about," she retorted indignantly pouring two cups and handing him one. "How could I be the cause of your troubles? What you are doing is attacking me instead of Irina. I think that's cowardly."

Drew's dark eyes gazed at her unperturbed.

"Do you never think of anyone but yourself?" he asked in an even voice.

Maggie could feel hot anger rising. If she didn't take a firm grip of herself she was going to do something she would regret. Why did he always have this effect on her, robbing her of her usual cool equilibrium.

"Hi!"

Julie came breezing in taking off her woollen hat so that her dark curls tumbled about her shoulders. "Bit of luck, got away early," she said as she sat down and the waitress brought an extra cup.

"Like old times, isn't it?" she said beaming at them over her tea. "Unfortunately I can't stay long I've got to see the wardrobe mistress. Poor Sandra's down with flu and I'm taking over her role in the new ballet; hence the costume alteration. Well, how's everyone?" she asked looking first at Drew and then Maggie.

"Everyone's fine." Maggie offered her a doughnut filled with jam.

"Thanks. I shouldn't really." Julie munched the doughnut happily for a few moments then looked across at Drew.

"I can't understand what's happened to Irina," she continued. "I remember seeing her in the hotel on the first day. Hope she isn't in serious trouble."

"What kind of trouble do you have

in mind?" Drew asked giving Julie his full attention. He'd always thought her a bit of a scatterbrain but she might know something.

"Well, I was thinking of defecting in reverse. Her father was Russian. Of course don't mention a word of this to anyone, it's just my idea and I could be dreadfully wrong."

Drew made no comment and Maggie looked ill at ease. If Irina has defected it's going to affect Drew's career, she thought anxiously.

"Where's Joel?" Julie asked brightly trying to change the mood.

"Sight-seeing with an American girl from his college," replied Maggie lamely.

"Oh I see," said Julie, puzzled but too polite to ask questions. "Got the wedding date fixed?"

"No, there's no date yet."

"I suppose you'll be getting married at Kingsley Magna," Julie continued gaily. "I always remember the Christmas parties there; Christmas Eve for the young ones and Boxing Day morning for the not so young. How's your father by the way," Julie added looking across at Drew.

"Very weak I'm afraid. He had another stroke a few months ago."

"I'm sorry to hear that. Do give him my kind regards."

The conversation then turned to the Lazonby Theatre company and Maggie's future plans.

"Actually I have no business being on holiday," said Maggie. "I should be in London trying to get a job."

"You'll get something," Julie comforted her. "I'm sure of it."

It was when Drew went to the cloakroom to collect his coat that Maggie got a chance to speak to Julie alone.

"Julie, you're an old friend and I'd like to confide in you. I'm not deliriously happy about marrying Joel. It's a peculiar feeling, I suppose I've got cold feet."

"A lot of people are like that," Julie

replied firmly. "You'll get over it. It will pass. You'll see I'm right."

"I hope you are," said Maggie fervently.

"Now there's a gorgeous hunk of man," said Julie lowering her voice as Drew approached. "But I never stood a chance."

"That's a serious look, Julie," he commented as they moved towards the entrance.

"Lost dreams are," she replied.

They left the hotel discussing a reunion when the tour finished, then Julie, waving goodbye hurried off in the direction of the theatre.

Maggie and Drew mingled for a few minutes with the fur-hatted crowd in the Stapana Stijna then turned off into a quiet side street. Soon they were in a labyrinth of quiet side streets and suddenly they saw the canals, intercrossing each other, the water rippling grey steel in the cold northern light. They paused a moment on an elegant stone bridge.

"Irina hasn't defected," Drew said quietly turning up the collar of his sheepskin coat as the breeze of the morning turned into a gale. "She likes the good things of the west too much."

"What do you think has happened to her?"

"I don't know," he said blowing on his hands. "Come on, let's get back — this wind's blowing from the Arctic. In a few more weeks these canals and the river will be frozen solid. Thank goodness we won't be here."

"Yes, but think of the skating. Every day you'd be able to practise and by the end of the winter you'd be very skilled."

They left the bridge and walked down a narrow side street.

"I've got more important things on my mind than skating." Drew looked at her over the top of his collar. "Maggie, what am I going to do? I told Ashley Morris I'd do my best to find her."

"The truth is we're helpless. We have nothing to go on."

They were passing a shop selling books and posters. Maggie announced she'd like to buy a poster. When she came out of the shop some five minutes later bearing one carrying the head of Lenin against a background of workers and the hammer and sickle there was a cold disapproving look in Drew's eyes.

"What did you buy that for?" he demanded sternly. "You had a choice of famous buildings or dancing peasants and you choose that!"

"It was just a bit of fun."

"All it's fit for is burning," Drew retorted savagely.

"What on earth is the matter with you?" demanded Maggie. "It's just an interesting souvenir of another culture."

"Is it?"

"Yes. And you're going neurotic."

"You know, Maggie, sometimes I think it would be better if you weren't here."

They walked on in silence Maggie stunned by his apparent unkindness, conscious of the wide mental gulf that separated them. They'd never been on the same wavelength. It was with relief when they met Bebe and Joel on the Dvocovy Bridge.

"What did Irina have to say?" asked Joel between gusts of wind as they buffeted their way across the bridge.

"She wasn't there," Drew replied tersely.

"You mean she's walked out," exclaimed Joel surprised. "She's going to be in trouble."

"Where did you go?" Maggie asked quickly to change the subject noticing Drew's heavily frowning face. The last thing he wanted was Joel's opinion on the situation.

"Tsar Peter's collection of rarities, curiosities and monsters," Bebe replied. "It was incredible. You should have come. After that we went to the university."

"What did you think of it?" Maggie asked turning to Joel.

"It's the one for me. Everyone I

spoke to couldn't have been nicer, particularly the tutors."

They crossed the road and entered the hotel. "All set for the opera tonight," Bebe asked looking at Maggie and Drew as she took off her expensive fur gloves.

"I'd forgotten all about it," said Maggie as they stepped into an empty lift.

"I won't be coming," announced Drew unexpectedly.

"Gee, why ever not?" Bebe looked disappointed.

"I have to work on a paper. I'm desperately behind."

"What about Nikolai? We're meeting him afterwards," Joel reminded him.

"Don't worry. I'll see you all after the performance."

The auditorium of the Opera House was breathtaking; filled with glittering chandeliers. They hung from the ceiling, at regular intervals along the edges of the balconies between golden cupids lying amongst golden foliage. It was even more beautiful than the Moscow theatre, thought Maggie.

The lights dimmed and the curtain rose on a stage packed with men and women in Oriental Russian costumes; the male singers big masculine bearded types and the women slim and beautiful with large soulful eyes.

In the second act dancing took over from the singing — dancing of wild abandonment, the men leaping into the air waving their swords whilst the music of Borodin rose and crashed in a welter of cymbals and brass.

In the interval Maggie, Joel and Bebe found an upper room, elegant and lined with mirrors where those of the audience who did not wish to take refreshments paraded in solemn twos and threes around the perimeter of the room. Maggie, Joel and Bebe joined the promenaders.

"It's straight out of Tolstoy," whispered Bebe excitedly.

"What do you know about Tolstoy?" Joel asked looking at her amused.

"I read him at high school," she replied defensively. "Of course that was before everything changed."

"What changed?" he asked, looking puzzled.

"My whole life. Dad found oil on our land. I'm going back years now."

There was silence for a few moments whilst Joel and Maggie adjusted to this. Then the bell rang and the intermission was over. They returned to their seats. Maggie wasn't really surprised. She had suspected something like that from the beginning. What kind of student wears mink?

When the opera finally finished and the leading soloists had taken their final bow, Joel, Maggie and Bebe made their way into the foyer and collected their coats from the attendant.

Nikolai and Drew were waiting for them; Drew having a contented expression on his face for once.

"Get a lot of work done?" Maggie asked as they moved out into the freezing night.

"Reasonably so."

"No work is more important that the opera," said Nikolai his small eyes bright as they passed beneath the light of a street lamp. "We now go to my brother Vladimir's apartment. He has recently been divorced and is glad of company."

They turned off into a small, poorly lit street and Maggie's feeling of unease returned despite the fact that Nikolai tried to disarm her by asking for her opinions on English life and English theatre. After what seemed like half an hour of walking through poorly lit narrow streets they finally entered an archway and found themselves in a dimly lit courtyard. Then into a dark doorway and up a spiral of stone steps. Nikolai stopped at a door and knocked.

It was opened by his brother, a younger, slimmer version of Nikolai who showed them into a warm, but shabby room. On the walls were remnants of a previous upper class life. There was a painting of a large house in the country and another of a woman in evening dress at the turn of the century in pale blue satin stitched with pearls, her shoulders bare, a fan in her hand.

Along one wall was a bed covered in a patchwork quilt, in the centre of the room a table of polished wood with chairs, and in the corner a record player with records of Abba and the Beatles, Nikolai's brother, Vladimir, had status.

Introductions were made. Bebe sat with Drew at the table and Maggie found herself next to Joel on the bed. Vodka was served in small wooden cups. A toast was drunk to friendship. Maggie took a small sip.

"No," said Nikolai. "You must drink vodka in one quick swallow. Like this."

He downed his drink in one gulp. Someone put on a record; "All the lonely people, where do they all come from . . ."

Maggie glanced around the room.

Yes, they were all lonely people. Vladimir and his recent divorce; Drew and his problems with an unfaithful wife; Bebe jilted by Guy. And suddenly she saw the reason why Joel had proposed to her. It had been out of sheer loneliness and for the same reason she had accepted.

"The Royal Westminster is in Leningrad," smiled Nikolai looking at Drew. "How is Irina? I presume you have seen her?"

"She's not with the company," Drew replied, a depressed expression on his face.

Nikolai looked puzzled. "I do not understand."

"Neither do I. She's somewhere in the country because she was seen in the Moscow hotel on the first day of the tour."

"Then she was not seen again?" asked Nikolai.

"That's right," replied Drew.

"This is very worrying," said Nikolai as he refilled everyone's wooden cup.

"What are you going to do?"

"Try to find her," replied Drew in a gloomy voice, "but I don't know where to start."

"When I met her in London," said Nikolai, "I remember her telling me about her father. He was a Russian refugee during the last war, and her grandmother Natasha Doestraskaya was a ballet dancer before the revolution."

"She often used to discuss her relations," said Joel. "In fact it was a bit of an obsession with her. I remember on one occasion she showed me old letters and photographs."

"Is this Irina's first visit to Russia?" Nikolai asked suddenly.

"Yes, it is," replied Drew giving Nikolai a curious look.

Nikolai slapped his knee. "That is what she has done. She has gone to find her relations. There are Doestraskayas at Golensk. Vassily is a director of the theatre there. One of them is a ballet dancer."

"Come to think of it," said Drew

slowly. "She once mentioned Golensk. An old uncle."

"I am right," Nikolai exclaimed delightedly. "I am certain of it. It is the most natural thing in the world to wish to see your cousins and aunts and uncles."

"At the expense of your career?" exclaimed Drew.

Nikolai held up his hand. "Something has happened to delay her. I am convinced of it. She may be ill." He turned to Drew. "I am going to Golensk during the next few days and shall make enquiries on your behalf."

"I'm very grateful to you," said Drew. "You are very kind."

"You are my friend. We have another vodka and this time we drink to Irina."

Everyone raised their wooden cups and drank. And suddenly Maggie had the curious feeling she didn't want Drew to find Irina. She couldn't analyse it because Drew either made her angry, miserable, never happy, so

185

it was certainly not because she wanted Drew's company.

"What's the matter, Maggie?" Joel slipped his arm around her waist. "I don't think you're enjoying this."

"Why do you say that?"

He cupped her chin in his hand. "Glum look on that pretty face. Come on, give me a smile."

Maggie smiled to please him.

"That's better. What happened this afternoon? When we met you on the bridge you weren't exactly the picture of happiness."

"Oh Drew was in one of his difficult moods," she said keeping her voice low.

"I couldn't understand why you went. You weren't avoiding me?"

"Don't be silly."

Drew glanced at his watch. "I think it's time we were going." He stood up. "Thanks for your hospitality and offer of help. We've had a wonderful evening and if ever you come to England . . . "

Everyone stood up and shook hands,

then Vladimir and Nikolai accompanied them through the quiet dark streets to the tram stop.

"I will telephone you as soon as possible," said Nikolai as the tram approached rumbling to a stop. The driver opened the automatic doors.

"Goodbye." Nikolai and Vladimir stood waving on the deserted pavement whilst they boarded the tram and fumbled for kopeks to insert in the ticket machine.

The tram rumbled off. It was crowded, mainly with evening workers going home who stared at them with unembarrassed curiosity. Joel was soon talking to an elderly woman. Maggie couldn't see Bebe as she stood strap hanging next to Drew.

"I wonder what Nikolai will have to say when he phones," Drew said reflectively as the tram lurched along.

"I don't trust him," said Maggie looking through the dark window opposite her.

"Why?" She turned to Drew. There

was a mocking glint in his eyes. "You know nothing about him," he continued.

"I know. It's something called feminine intuition."

"Could we have some logical thinking for a change," Drew demanded exasperatedly.

The tram suddenly came to a halt throwing Maggie against Drew who steadied her by putting his arm round her drawing her close to him. His lips were very close. Too close she decided and struggled to move away but Drew held her all the tighter.

"Don't worry," he whispered. "I wouldn't dream of kissing you in public. The Russians are very sensitive about such matters."

"Has it occurred to you, you might not get the chance."

"Will you never change."

The tram doors opened and people started pushing past them to the exit.

"Hey, this is our stop," called Joel pushing his way between them with

Bebe following close behind.

They alighted from the tram, crossed to the pavement, then turned the corner of the street. A cold wind blew from the river, and in the darkness the lights from their ultra-modern hotel glittered.

Mr Collins met them in the foyer and a long discussion ensued on the merits of Russian opera. After a while Maggie made her excuses and went up to her room. To her surprise her door was not closed — she must have been in a hurry to get to the theatre. It was of little importance; all her valuables were in her handbag.

In the privacy of her room she found she was still smarting from Drew's unkind remark outside the poster shop. How cruel can you get she thought as she got undressed, then went into the bathroom and before the mirror went through the ritual of applying cleansing cream, skin tonic, skin food. It was a soothing exercise, relaxed her, not that it did much good. The set had been a

Christmas present from one of the girls at the theatre. Sweet of Lisa to buy it for her anyway.

She walked through into the bedroom and got into bed, switching off the main light but keeping the bedside lamp on. She was thinking of Irina. She didn't care very much for the woman but at the same time she hoped nothing terrible had happened to her, and as for defecting that seemed too crazy for words.

Sleep seemed far away so opening a light novel she had brought for such an occasion she turned to the first page and started reading. She had hardly read the first paragraph when she heard the noise. It was a small sound that seemed to come from the wardrobe cupboard. Suddenly the door started to open.

9

A YOUNG, blond man stepped out of the wardrobe, and as Maggie stared at his flushed face a shiver of fear ran through her, sharp and unpleasant like an electric shock.

He's been drinking was her first thought as he paused leering at her, taking in her low-cut nightgown, the soft curve of her breasts. Then as he staggered towards her, muttering something in an Eastern European language, his eyes full of lust, she sprang into action hurling her book at him, catching him smartly on the forehead.

He let out a cry of anger and paused to rub his head. Maggie leapt out of bed and made for the door. But she wasn't quite fast enough, as she fled past him his fingers caught the flowing fabric of her nightgown.

He gave an excited shout. Maggie spun round, seeing a pot of face cream on the dressing-table threw it at him hitting him full in the face. He released his grip, an ugly expression on his face whilst Maggie pushed an armchair between them then ran the remaining short passage to the door, opened it and fled into the deserted corridor.

The floor lady's desk was masked by a large potted palm. Drew's room was opposite. She had no alternative but to ask him for protection; so running across the corridor she hammered on the door.

"Drew! Open the door, quick!" she shouted. She didn't care if she wakened the whole corridor. That embarrassment was nothing compared to the fate that obviously awaited her in her room. She glanced nervously back at her door. She had only partly closed it and as yet there was no sign of the man.

She was just about to repeat her

knocking when Drew opened the door standing there in black pyjamas blinking sleepily at her.

"I never expected this Maggie," he smiling curiously at her as she fled past him into the room.

"There's a man in my room," she gasped. "He was going to rape me."

Drew closed the door and followed her into the room.

"They all say that." There was a teasing note in his voice.

"I'm telling the truth," she protested. "It was the most horrible experience of my life."

Her eyes filled with tears. The delayed reaction of shock was setting in. She started shaking from head to foot.

"What you need is a brandy," said Drew taking a bottle and glass out of his case and pouring a measure. "I always keep a bottle with me in case of emergencies like this. Now tell me all about it."

He led her to the settee and they

sat down. Maggie took a gulp of the fiery liquid. "He was hiding in the wardrobe." Her voice was a whisper and her hand holding the glass was shaking so much she had to put it down then held both her hands together.

"I was in such a hurry to get to the theatre I didn't close my door — that's how he got in."

"I hope you learn a lesson from this. Who is he? Do you know him?"

"I think he's one of the Finns who arrived today. He was drunk of course."

Drew stood up and put on his dressing-gown.

"Where are you going?" asked Maggie wide-eyed with fear. "Don't leave me."

"I'm going to deal with your intruder and throw him out of your room."

"Be careful Drew," she warned. "He could get nasty."

"Don't worry about me. If he's drunk, I've got the advantage over him."

Drew went out closing the door behind him. Maggie continued sitting on the settee sipping the brandy, longing for his return, praying the confrontation would not deteriorate into a brawl that would necessitate the manager being called. A minute later there was a knock at the door.

"Maggie!" came Drew's voice. "It's me."

She opened the door cautiously a few inches. Drew was standing there looking very calm, not a hair out of place.

"Come on, aren't you going to let me in?"

Maggie held back the door and Drew entered.

"What happened?" she asked fearfully.

"Nothing," came the reply. "There's no one there. Your room's empty. Sure you didn't dream it up?"

Drew took off his dressing-gown and flung it over the back of a chair.

"Why on earth should I do such a thing?" She felt hurt and indignant he could have thought her capable of such action.

"I wouldn't put it past you."

"That was a nasty remark, or shall I say a very conceited one. You really think I'd go to all the trouble of rushing across to your room with the manufactured story of an attempted rape. My God, you've got a big opinion of yourself."

A slow smile spread across Drew's face. "Not in the least. Just worldly wise." He pulled Maggie to her feet.

"So you really think I'm that type . . . " Maggie began. Drew's arms tightened around her and she could feel his strong thighs pressing against hers.

"What type?" he whispered in a teasing voice, his lips on her neck.

"The type that will do anything to get a man."

"Well, aren't you?"

"How dare you!" Maggie panted as she struggled to free herself from Drew's suffocating embrace, but the more she struggling the more Drew tightened his grip. Finally they both lost their balance and fell on the floor. Through the partly drawn curtain a shaft of pure ethereal moonlight drifted and swam giving Maggie's face a luminous glow.

"Russian moonlight has a special quality," Drew whispered in Maggie's ear. "It transforms ordinary mortals into magical beings. I love you Maggie; I always have." His hands closed over her breasts.

"Leave me alone, Drew." But it was a feeble protest for the magic was touching Maggie as Drew commenced to kiss her; slow, sensuous kissing that sent a flame coursing through her veins. Then Drew's lips moved to her throat to start the downward journey to the hollow between her breasts.

"We shouldn't be doing this," Maggie whispered in an awed voice; everything seemed unreal, dreamlike.

"Why not?" came Drew's reply. "You want me."

"I don't," she replied, her voice uncertain.

"You're lying."

"I'm not."

But Maggie knew it was true for her whole body was aching for him. It was almost a physical pain.

"Let me make love to you," Drew whispered. "It's the least you can do considering you ruined my life."

Maggie sat bolt upright. "Did I hear correctly? I ruined your life? Have you gone mad?"

He gave a sad smile. "I only married Irina because I couldn't have you."

The mist cleared from her brain. "You mean the day before I left for Cumbria . . . in the meadow . . . " Then she put her hands to her face and laughed gently.

"What's the matter?" Drew asked wanting to be let in on the joke.

"I thought you wanted me to be your mistress."

Drew smiled as he took Maggie in his arms. "For so grossly misjudging me, you really ought to make it up to me."

198

"And why should I?" she asked provocatively folding her arms over her breasts. Drew grasped her roughly and pushed her back onto the floor, then slipped her shoulder straps down so that her white breasts were revealed in all their beauty.

His fingers started slowly and gently to caress her nipples. When they stood upright, pert and eager she cried to him to stop. But the weakness was coming, and the pain, and the sense of intoxication. Then she was drifting, flying, in a moon-drenched world, her being filled with joy, a joy that grew to such intensity she was a disembodied spirit soaring to the stars.

Later she felt Drew pick her up and carry her to his bed. There she slept. When she awoke it was early. Drew was still asleep in the other bed. She lay a moment feeling deliciously contented. Looking across at his tousled head on the pillow, the events of the previous evening seemed an incredible magical dream. She loved Drew and he loved her. He had always loved her but she had been too blind to see it.

Then suddenly she thought of Joel — sweet blind Joel, who believed she was going to marry him. Her sense of guilt was heavy indeed. Then she thought of Irina. Drew was still married to her, and for a moment she felt quite ill.

The first thing to do is to break off the engagement to Joel, she thought firmly as she got out of bed, and secondly if Drew failed to find Irina they would just have to wait a long time for the divorce.

She walked across and kissed Drew on the forehead. He stirred and turned over flinging his arm across the pillow. Maggie gave him a soft smile. She must get back to her room and dress but where was her room key? Drew had put it down somewhere last night and it seemed a pity to waken him. After a considerable amount of searching she discovered it on top of the television set.

Opening the door she tiptoed across the empty corridor and back into her own room. In daylight she felt no fear. Keeping the outer door open as a temporary safeguard she flung back the bathroom door, the wardrobe door, got down on her hands and knees and looked beneath the bed. She was alone. Never again would she leave her door unlocked. On the other hand if she had . . .

She smiled whimsically to herself as she bathed and dressed, musing to herself how strange life could be. What sudden twists and turns it could take. She dressed with care in a fine worsted check suit and black sweater; in the mirror her eyes were shining.

She caught sight of Drew as soon as she entered the dining-room. A quiver of excitement shot through her, she felt herself blushing as she sat down in the empty seat next to him. Is this what it is like to be in love? He turned to her, his eyes warm and loving.

"No more trouble?" he asked softly as he poured her a cup of coffee.

"No," she smiled.

"If it happens again, just come and see me."

"Thanks."

His eyes lingered over her lovingly, admiringly. It was like reclining in a gorgeous scented bath. Drew loved her, Maggie Kerr, daughter of his ex-manager, now an out-of-work actress, and likely to remain that way. It was unbelievable.

"What are you doing this morning, Drew?" she asked buttering a roll and taking a bite.

"Continuing on my paper," he answered. "I've got to present it the first of next month so I haven't much time left. It's very important. You'll have to be patient with me."

"I'll be patient."

Maggie glanced around the table. What a relief Joel was not there. Never in all the years she had known Joel had he had such an effect on her as

Drew had had last night. She dreaded their next meeting for she knew Joel's subsequent unhappiness would affect her.

"What are you going to do, Maggie?" Drew asked folding up his serviette.

"Haven't decided," she smiled.

"Well, whatever it is have a good morning and see you at lunch."

Maggie decided to visit the Wedding Palace. It was a small party that mounted the staircase. In the main hall could be heard the melodic strains of Tchaikovsky's Piano Concerto No. 1., and beneath the chandeliers the wedding couples were waiting, the women carrying bouquets of gladioli and the men ill-at-ease with a flower in their button hole.

She was thankful that Joel, Drew and Bebe had not wanted to come. She needed a period of peace, to be alone. Everytime she thought of Drew's love for her, it was like bringing out a secret treasure and looking at it in wonder. But it wouldn't be secret for long, for today she would have to tell Joel. And every time she thought of Joel she was filled with guilt and sorrow.

One by one the couples moved into the Registry Hall. Here Mozart's 'Jupiter' Symphony played. As Drew would be a divorced man their wedding would have to take place in a Registry Office. She would miss a church wedding. Then suddenly she remembered they could have a church blessing — perhaps it could take place in the chapel in Kingsley Magna Hall. She would be able to wear the traditional wedding dress and veil, so it wouldn't be so bad.

When the couples were pronounced man and wife the music changed to Rachmaninoff. They signed the register, exchanged rings and it was over. There were stars in their eyes and Maggie felt she shared their happiness, she too had made the right choice.

Back at the hotel she made for the

tea room and ordered tea together with thick slices of cake full of fruit and nuts. She should have gone into the dining-room with the rest of the party but somehow the feeling of wanting to be alone still lingered. On a video she watched Ukrainian boys and girls dancing in national costume. The door opened and Drew hurried in.

"I've been looking for you everywhere," he exclaimed sitting on the bench opposite her. "I've just had a phone call from Nikolai. He's asked me to go with him to Golensk this afternoon. He's been making enquiries and he feels certain she must be there. I'll be able to talk to her. There's nothing worse than a dead marriage hovering over one's head. Then I'll be able to see my solicitor when I get back and get things moving."

He looked so happy, so eager to go, but Maggie had to say it.

"Why is Nikolai going out of his way to help you?"

"He's not," Drew protested. "He was

going there anyway. Now stop being so suspicious."

They took the lift down to the ground floor, and stood in the wide foyer with its view of the river. Drew looked at his watch.

"I must dash, Maggie. I'm meeting Nikolai at the station. Wish me luck."

He kissed her on the lips and was gone, out through the swing doors and into a waiting taxi. Maggie turned away with an appalling sense of desolation.

For something to do she went into the Berioska shop and bought a record of Russian folk music. Anything to pass the time, to stop her from thinking. As she came out she almost bumped into Mr Collins.

"Hello, Maggie. Enjoying Leningrad?" he asked a smile on his jovial face.

"Unforgettable," she replied trying to make the comment sound casual.

"Where are your friends?" he continued as they strolled across the hotel foyer.

"Drew has just gone to Golensk,"

she replied in a miserable voice.

"Golensk!" he exclaimed in consternation. "What on earth possessed him to go there?"

"He thinks his wife is in Golensk. He has to see her very urgently."

Mr Collins' look of consternation increased. "But Golensk is a hundred kilometres from here."

"Is that important?" Maggie asked innocently.

"I'll say it is," Mr Collins replied sternly. "He's just gone into a forbidden zone."

Maggie suddenly went cold. "How serious is that?"

"Couldn't be worse. If he's caught he'll be arrested. Of course Intourist would help him . . ."

"Arrested! I've got to stop him. He's going by train; left about half an hour ago."

Maggie hurried across to the receptionist. Leningrad had several railway stations.

"Will you telephone for a taxi," she

instructed the young woman. "I want the railway station for the Golensk train."

The call was made, then Mr Collins accompanied Maggie to the main entrance to watch for the arrival of the taxi.

"British tourists make this mistake from time to time," commented Mr Collins. "We are so used to living in a free country where we can travel unhindered by regulations."

The dark-coloured Volga drew up at the hotel entrance. Maggie bid Mr Collins goodbye, then hurried out into the icy atmosphere.

In his haste to see Irina, Drew had forgotten all about forbidden zones, thought Maggie as the taxi moved off, along the embankment, then over the bridge. Nikolai must have known, her thoughts continued, or was that the whole point of the exercise.

Every time the taxi stopped at the lights Maggie sat seething with impatience, a desperation rising within her. Then a terrible thought struck her, what should she do if she couldn't find Drew at the station, or the train had already left?

When the taxi finally stopped outside the station building, the driver turned and looked at her enquiringly.

"Wait. *Padazh*."

Then opening the door she ran into the station entrance. There was no sign of Drew or Nikolai amongst the small knots of people standing around. Which platform for the Golensk train she thought desperately. She hurried to a man in an official-looking uniform not sure whether he was a station employee or a naval officer in his dark clothes and gold braiding.

"Golensk?" she asked him, speaking as clearly as she could.

Thankfully he understood and pointed to the platform immediately beyond the ticket barrier. There was no one at the barrier so Maggie ran through unhindered to the waiting train. Luggage was still being loaded into the luggage van, and people were standing at open doors saying goodbye.

She half ran half walked along the platform, her eyes searching every window, every open door. She remembered Drew was wearing his English sheepskin coat. Please God she prayed, let me find him, and suddenly there he was, stepping off the end coach to take a photograph.

"Drew!" she yelled with joy and relief.

He turned immediately and his eyes lit up at the sight of her.

"Maggie," he called. "What are you doing here?"

She ran to him, clutching his arm breathlessly. "Don't go to Golensk. It's a forbidden zone. Mr Collins said you'd get arrested."

The smile was whipped from Drew's face. "A forbidden zone! How could I be so stupid. All I could think of was Irina . . ."

A whistle blew and doors banged,

then as the train started to move Nikolai appeared at a door and lowered the window.

"What happened?" he called.

"I'm not coming," Drew called back.

Nikolai's reply was lost as the train gathered speed as it left the station and the last they saw of him was his angry face leaning out of the window.

10

AS the train disappeared from view, Drew turned to Maggie and his face creased into a broad smile.

"What would I do without you, Maggie? Forgetting forbidden zones. Running the risk of being arrested."

They started walking along the empty platform towards the exit. What a wonderful feeling, thought Maggie to be needed by the man you love.

"What made you think of forbidden zones?" Drew continued taking her arm. Maggie turned and smiled at him.

"Mr Collins told me."

"During a history lecture."

"There was no lecture."

"I'm very grateful to him and must thank him when we get back."

They were now outside the station

building and Maggie waved to the waiting taxi driver.

"Even a taxi's waiting," exclaimed Drew as they walked across. "You think of everything." Maggie flushed with pleasure as they got in and set off.

"Well I'll just have to face facts," said Drew leaning back in the seat, "my mission has failed. I came to Russia to discuss a divorce with Irina so that I could get the whole miserable business over and done with and get a new life started." His hand slipped into Maggie's. "Now it's not going to happen. We must be patient. There's always desertion but that will take years."

Maggie sat beside him feeling surprisingly unperturbed. She was confident in their love for each other. The years would soon pass and one day they would look back on this difficult time nostalgically.

"I can wait," she said simply.

Drew gently brushed a kiss against her mouth.

"There's no one quite like you and never has been."

There was an excited tremor in Maggie's stomach as she leaned her head against Drew's shoulder. She had never been so happy, felt such utter bliss. Then she thought of what might have happened if she had missed the train.

"Nikolai's no friend of yours," she commented keeping her voice low. "He must have known going to Golensk, you were likely to get into trouble with the authorities."

"But why?" asked Drew raising his eyebrows. "Blackmail?"

"I think so."

"He knows nothing about me."

"He knows Irina. She could have discussed you without thinking of the consequences."

The taxi stopped outside the hotel and Drew and Maggie got out, paid the driver and climbed the steps. An icy wind was blowing from the river. Maggie shivered.

"The sooner we leave Russia the better," said Drew turning up his collar.

"If I ever come here again, I shall buy one of those fur-lined leather coats," announced Maggie opening the swing doors.

"And a silver fox hat," added Drew, a warm glow in his dark eyes as he followed her into the foyer. "And all the men in Russia will fall in love with you."

Maggie laughed. "I don't want all the men in Russia to fall in love with me." Just you, she thought looking at Drew, Just you.

They walked past the armed guard. "Won't it be wonderful," said Maggie in a bare whisper, "to be back in a sane country."

Drew nodded. "Let's have a drink to celebrate. I feel I've been dragged from the edge of a precipice."

Over a glass of white wine in the little bar on the ground floor, against a background of taped balalaika music,

Drew discussed his future plans for Kingsley Magna, and as Maggie looked into his strong masculine face, that firm yet sensitive mouth she knew so well where her future lay. She must have always known it deep in her subconscious mind. That was why she had always been so hypersensitive about him. His acceptance of her had always been of the utmost importance.

Then she thought of Joel and felt utterly wretched. She could now see so clearly it was a brother-sister affection that in time would grow to boredom. How could she have been so thoughtless?

"Sometimes I wonder if I should give up my job and devote all my time to running the estate," Drew was saying. "Actually Father never wanted me to do anything else, and I think it was a great disappointment when I told him I was interested in electronics."

"It wouldn't work out," Maggie exclaimed vehemently. "You'd be bored within a month. It wouldn't be challenging enough for you. Going to market, buying and selling cattle, working out feeding schedules, making the decision when to sell."

Drew grinned at her. "You weren't an estate manager's daughter for nothing. I think I'll just have to concentrate on persuading your father to come back." Then he took Maggie's hand in his. "Legally I'm going to be married to Irina for a long time to come and I can offer you nothing except my love."

There was a burning sensation in Maggie's eyes and a lump rose in her throat.

"That's good enough for me," she said in a small voice.

"What's the position between you and Joel?"

"I'm speaking to him today. Oh Drew, it's all been such a dreadful mistake — getting engaged to Joel. He's going on the Tretyakov tour this afternoon and I only hope Bebe keeps out of the way for some of the time. Why do we make such stupid mistakes in life? Sometimes I can't understand myself."

"We do things for the wrong reasons," Drew suggested.

"Probably." Maggie took a quick glance at her watch. "I'll have to dash. The bus leaves in ten minutes."

Drew accompanied Maggie up the carpeted stairs and into the foyer now filled with a busy throng of people. Maggie saw Joel straight away, talking to Greisha. She'd have to wait for a quiet moment in the Tretyakov Palace.

Suddenly through the main swing doors came a woman. She was beautiful with high cheek bones, a flawless complexion, large grey eyes, her dark hair swept up behind her head, and on her head was perched a mink hat like a large powder puff.

It was Irina!

Maggie felt a deadening of her senses, a fatalistic feel of doom as she watched Irina searching the crowd, then her eyes alighting on Drew walked towards him.

"Darling!" She held out her arms and embraced him planting a kiss on his cheek. There was a whiff of expensive perfume.

"And you too, Maggie! What a surprise!" Her lips brushed against Maggie's cheek. "What are you doing in Leningrad? I was so surprised when Ashley said you were here."

"Looking for you Irina." Drew stared at her with a hard glint in his eyes.

"Me? How flattering. What have I done to deserve such attention?" She fluttered her long eyelashes at him.

"We need somewhere private where we can talk. I can only think of my room." Drew's voice was gruff, impatient.

"Hello Irina," hailed Joel as he approached. "Drew's been searching Moscow and Leningrad for you."

"So I hear."

"Hi!" said Bebe appearing from nowhere. "Could I have your autograph. It will make the girls back home absolutely green." She thrust a book and pen into Irina's hands.

Drew moved away in the direction of the lifts. "Are you coming, Irina?" he called impatiently.

Irina signed Bebe's book then hurried after Drew. Joel turned to Maggie.

"Where've you been?" he demanded. "You missed lunch. I phoned your room twice."

"I'm sorry, Joel. But I've been busy extricating Drew out of possible trouble." She then proceeded to tell him about Drew wanting to go to Golensk. She was still relating the story when they got on the Intourist bus. Joel sat next to her and Bebe sat in front with Mr Collins. The bus moved off and Greisha stood up microphone in hand.

"I will now give you some more facts about life in the U.S.S.R." she announced. "Twenty roubles a month is the average rent for an apartment. This includes heating, water and local telephone . . . " It was like listening to a recording.

"How did you like the Wedding Palace?" Joel whispered in Maggie's ear.

"Very impersonal business," she replied with a wistful smile. "The brides and grooms were almost on conveyor belts. Joel, I want to talk to you . . . " she began diffidently.

But Joel wasn't listening. "Bebe asked me to take a boat trip with her. That was one of the worst decisions of the holiday. I have never been so cold. As soon as I got back I had to go under a hot shower. A better bet would have been one of the museums, at least they would have been warm."

Joel was talking rapidly about everything except the one thing that was uppermost in his mind. He was a man in a panic grasping at straws. At last Maggie could stand it no longer.

"Joel, it's not working out — is it — you and me."

"My God Maggie, how could you do it?"

221

"I was just going to tell you . . . "
Maggie began but Joel interrupted her.

"You and Drew have double-crossed me right through this holiday. Then last night you went to his room to sleep with him. I saw you running back to your room this morning, you didn't even have the modesty to wear a dressing-gown." Joel's cheeks were flushed and he held his mouth in a tight angry line.

Maggie protested, tears in her eyes. "Stop it, Joel. You don't understand. There had been no double-crossing on this holiday right up to last night. I had been true to you. Then last night a drunken Finn got into my room. You see I'd forgotten to close my door when I went to the theatre . . . "

But Joel didn't want to know the details and interrupted again. "My door is only two down from you. You went to Drew because he's the man you are always thinking about . . . "

At this point Mr Collins turned

round and Maggie hastened to dry her tears.

"Have you read about the siege of Leningrad?" he enquired with a soft smile.

Maggie shook her head. "Lasted nine hundred days," he continued. "The German army had encircled the city. There was no electricity, gas or running water. They burnt their furniture to keep warm, they ate wallpaper and rubber . . ."

"Certainly puts your own problems into their right perspective," commented Bebe.

Leningrad had now been left behind and they were in open country, but a countryside that was puzzling for all the fields were glassed in, in long rows in every direction to the horizon. Mr Collins seeing their perplexed looks put them right as usual.

"With a summer that lasts three months," he explained, "it's the only way to grow vegetables."

Joel sat gazing through the window

in stubborn silence.

"I'm sorry, Joel," whispered Maggie. "Sorry for everything."

The bus now entered a village street of simple wooden houses and a few minutes later entered through a pair of massive wrought-iron gates. At the end of the long drive it stopped in a courtyard surrounded by stables and coach-houses.

As the party left the bus an icy blast of wind buffeted them through an archway and there before them lay the Tretyakov Palace, sumptuous in its eighteenth-century splendour of heavily encrusted ornamentation. At the southern end a cluster of golden domes rose up at roof level.

"Makes you think of a wedding cake," said Bebe as they entered by a door in the northern wing.

In a golden room where golden leaves smothered the walls, encircled the mirrors, sprinkled the chandeliers, played games around the ceiling murals, Joel walked up to Maggie.

"You're a fool Maggie, just like all the rest."

"What do you mean? All the rest?"

"Look, I know as well as anyone that Drew's marriage has been going through a rough patch. The long periods when Irina's been away — sometimes he got bored."

"I don't want to listen," she protested turning away.

"You'll have to," he said placing his hand on her arm. "Whether you like it or not. Drew's here to affect a reconciliation. Divorce is the last thing he wants. Didn't you see the way he looked at her?"

"He was glad the painful business would soon be over."

Joel was making her feel unpleasantly uncomfortable, tugging at the protective cloak she hugged around herself. "Look Joel, I don't want to talk about Irina and Drew."

"Why, because the truth hurts?" he asked spitefully. "Drew's been using you."

"Why are you talking to me like this?" demanded Maggie, her eyes blazing.

"Because we have to," he replied sternly. "We've got to clear things up between you and me. From the night in Moscow when you went on a private errand for Drew I knew it was all up between you and me. So I turned to Bebe for consolation."

"So it's all my fault," she exclaimed hotly, tears spilling down her cheeks.

"Not really, Maggie," said Joel suddenly looking crestfallen. "It's a long story — connected with Bebe. You see I fell for her right at the beginning of the course but I didn't exist. All she could see was Guy. And when she moved in with him I was shattered. I thought that was the end of Bebe. Then in the early autumn Guy asked if I'd like to make up a foursome and go to Russia. You know the rest."

Maggie gave a sad smile. "It was inevitable. I'm sorry Joel that you're the loser out of this. I take it Bebe's still in love with Guy?"

"Not exactly." Joel was now looking very sheepish. "Bebe has realised what a terrible mistake she has made. It's me she really wants."

Maggie was about to make a polite comment when Joel cut in. He was the one now with a guilty conscience.

"Don't be angry, Maggie. I know I haven't been honest with you, but let's be sensible and remain friends. You know with you and me it's never been that wild crazy feeling that starts in the pit of your stomach and you feel you'll just die if you don't see her again."

"It's like that with you and Bebe?"

Joel nodded. "You and I have always been good friends and nothing can ever change that. But right now I don't want my big brother hurting you and he's quite capable of that. He hasn't changed except in a superficial way. He'll only want you if he can't get Irina back. So be on your guard."

Joel glanced around the large empty

room. "Hey, we've been left behind and I don't fancy walking back to Leningrad."

It took them thirty minutes to find their tour party in the one hundred and fifty roomed palace. Maggie was glad she had had the talk with Joel even though parts of it had been painful, and she did not agree with his criticism of Drew nor the reason why he had come to Russia. Poor Joel, he hadn't the faintest conception of the love Drew had for her.

As they left the palace it started to snow, large fluffy flakes that melted when they touched the ground. Bebe held her hands up like a child to catch them.

"Gee, it's just like Christmas," she cried as Joel took her picture before they boarded the bus. All the way back to Leningrad, Maggie was thinking of Drew. There would have been angry exchanges but by now everything would have been settled. She was so eager to see him again because now she was a totally free woman, all her commitments had gone and he would be deciding which solicitor should deal with the case.

She was filled with a sense of elation as she went up in the lift and along the corridor. When she reached Drew's door she knocked. No one came. He was probably in the bar or dining-room. She waited in her room an hour for Drew to phone then finally feeling hungry went down to the dining-room.

A dozen times during the meal Maggie could not control the impulse to glance across to the entrance in the hope of catching sight of his tall familiar figure. He did not come.

"Got a date with Drew tonight?" asked Bebe sipping her coffee.

"I haven't actually. He's working on a paper. He's very busy." Maggie tried to be as nonchalant as she could conscious of Joel overhearing the conversation.

"Tough. Fancy an evening of Georgian dancing. We saw it advertised in a little theatre next to the hotel. Well Greisha had to translate for us. While we're here I want to soak up everything Russian."

Maggie went with them. Better than sitting alone in her room, waiting for the phone that never rang, thinking excruciating thoughts. So sitting there in the darkened auditorium watching the lovely Georgian women in their pale saffron gowns and long black pigtails gliding across the stage to the delicate tinkling music it was inevitable she would think of Drew and Irina.

Where were they? She hadn't seen them for five hours. Surely you have said all you want to say in half that time. Was Joel right that the purpose of meeting was to affect a reconciliation? Her confidence was now starting to fray around the edges. Irina was a strong personality. She manipulated people. Was she manipulating Drew right now?

Her spirits were low as the show came to an end and the lights came on.

"Like to go for a drink in that bar

230

across the street," suggested Joel as they left the theatre and stood shivering in the freezing darkness. It seemed a good idea so they hurried across and entered what seemed to be a reconstruction of old China, taking their seats at the bar amidst red lacquer bamboo and Chinese lanterns. The barman though was a high cheek-boned Slavonic-looking man. Joel ordered vodkas.

"A lot of nonsense has been written about vodka," announced Joel. "But the truth is, it has been more thoroughly filtered than any whisky or gin. Vodka is in fact one of the gentlest drinks known to man . . . "

In the dimly lit bar a couple sat drinking in the far corner.

"And as Nikolai said," Joel continued, "taken in one quick swallow; and the custom is to follow it with a bit of salt herring or caviar. Many Russians drink mineral water alternately with their vodka, this way you never get a hang-over . . . "

Now that she had had a talk with

Joel that awful sense of guilt had gone. She felt at ease with him, just like she used to, but now there was a new kind of relationship, one not marred by any emotional problems.

The couple in the corner got up and started moving towards the bar.

It was Drew and Irina!

11

AS Drew and Irina approached, Irina started to weep uncontrollably wiping her tears with a white lace handkerchief. Drew taut and pale took her arm.

"Let me buy you a drink," suggested Joel sympathetically, looking at Irina.

"No thanks," Drew replied hurriedly. "We have to go." Then he looked at Maggie and in his eyes was a look of defeat. "I'll ring you," he mouthed the words and Maggie, suffocating with guilt, remorse, turned away, only to see Drew and Irina's reflection in the mirror behind the bar as they moved away and left through the curtained doorway.

Joel gave a low whistle. "Has Drew got problems," he murmured seeing the tragic expression on Maggie's face. "Well, I did warn you," he continued,

233

"and Irina's a clever woman. I reckon she knows about you that's why she put on the weeping act just now. Drew is putty in her hands."

Maggie downed the vodka in one and shuddered.

"Like another?" asked Joel. "There's nothing like getting stoned."

"No thanks," snapped Maggie. "I don't solve my problems by getting tight."

"All right. I was only trying to help."

To fill the awkward silence Bebe started talking about the family summer house on the Connecticut coast.

"It's quite small really," she explained. "It only has sixteen rooms and life there is very informal. We spend most of our time on the beach . . ."

During a suitable pause Maggie made her excuses and left. The snow had stopped and lay in a thin carpet on the deserted pavement. Overhead the velvet darkness was filled with stars, and suddenly she thought of Mirbeck Moor and the roaring torrent in the valley and in the distance the blue fells.

Maggie made up her mind. In the hotel foyer the first person she saw was Greisha, standing by the receptionist desk talking to a clerk.

"Is there any chance of getting a seat on tomorrow's plane for London?" Maggie asked politely a smile on her lips. She was asking the impossible but you never knew your luck.

Greisha looked at Maggie wearily. "Is it urgent? You are booked for the Saturday flight."

I've just broken off my engagement, allowed myself to be seduced by a married man who is now back with his wife.

"Yes it is urgent."

"I'll phone the airport," said Greisha commencing to dial the number. "But it won't be easy."

"Thanks."

Greisha talked to first one airport official then another, then suddenly she turned to Maggie. "You are fortunate.

There is an empty seat on tomorrow's flight, but the plane leaves at nine which means a very early start catching the airport bus at seven."

"I'll be down long before then," said Maggie. "Thanks again and I'm sorry for the trouble I've caused."

"There is no trouble. You will come back to Russia?"

Maggie smiled bravely. "Perhaps."

And all the way up in the lift Maggie knew she would never come back. She was running and she wouldn't stop until she reached home.

In her room she packed her bag, set her travelling alarm clock, undressed and got into bed. Then she lay there waiting for the phone to ring, and as her little clock ticked away the minutes and the minutes became an hour she knew he would never ring. Finally drowsiness overcame her and she fell asleep.

She awoke to hear the pinging of her alarm. It was 6.15 a.m. She got out of bed and pulled back the curtain. The stars were still shining and overhead she could just make out the Plough and Pole star.

Drew hadn't phoned last night. She was forgotten, now that he was with Irina and she could feel nothing but bitterness towards him and anger towards herself. How could she have been such a fool to allow herself to be manoeuvred into the position of the other woman. She was glad it was an early start; there would be no embarrassing explanations and goodbyes. She would just steal away and disappear.

At the airport there was an excruciating two-hour wait. There was still time for Drew to phone, thought Maggie, as she waited in the tiny departure lounge. Surely he would make enquiries and Greisha would tell him but no voice over the loudspeaker system announced a phone call for her.

When the plane finally took off, Maggie knew it was all over and all the way back to England she was on a wavelength of misery and humiliation. Drew had used her and Joel had been so right. *He'll only want you if he can't get Irina back.* She'd lost and the only thing left was to be a good loser.

At Gatwick she had a cup of coffee realising she had to go to Kingsley Magna to pick up her car. That was a crazy idea. She should have gone straight to Gatwick and met them there instead of leaving her car in the Midlands and travelling in the Brooksbys' car.

She wasn't feeling very happy by the time she arrived at Kingsley Magna. Mrs Meeson greeted her kindly, looking keenly at her dispirited tired face.

"I knew you wouldn't like it there," she said showing Maggie into her private sitting-room. "Have a meal with me here and then it's straight to bed. You look exhausted."

Maggie felt too tired and low-spirited to protest.

"Where's Drew and Joel and that American girl?" Mrs Meeson asked as she placed a bowl of hot soup before Maggie.

"They're still in Russia — I changed my plans," said Maggie. "There wasn't much point in prolonging the agony."

"I don't blame you. Having that there K.G.B. following you around everywhere."

"It's nothing to do with that," said Maggie irritably. Mrs Meeson looked at her closely. "Why don't you phone your Dad now that you're back."

When the meal finished Maggie went into the Tapestry Room and dialled Mirbeck. There was no reply.

"Happen he's gone down to your local," suggested Mrs Meeson. "He always liked a beer of an evening."

"Possibly," Maggie replied. She was now more impatient than ever to get home.

Mrs Meeson took her upstairs and showed her into a guest room. It was small and comfortable. Maggie put her bag down and went across and drew the curtains. Mrs Meeson walked across to the bed. It was very old with a high-canopied bedhead.

"Drew always liked this bed," she said with a satisfied tone in her voice. "He used to tell me it was made of wood from the Spanish Armada." Then she paused and smiled, "He'd tell you anything and get away with it."

Maggie felt a lump rise in her throat and she could keep her unhappiness from Mrs Meeson no longer. She gave a choking sound as the tears started, growing in intensity as all the pent-up misery broke forth.

"There, there my girl," consoled Mrs Meeson. "I know what's happened. You and Joel have quarrelled. If you take the advice of an old woman you'll make it up with him. Now have a good night's sleep and in the morning things won't be so bad as they seem."

Maggie dried her tears and when Mrs Meeson had left the room she prepared for bed. Mrs Meeson was right. A good night's sleep did wonders for one's spirits. But as soon as Maggie got into bed her eyes filled with tears and the weeping started afresh, finally falling asleep through sheer exhaustion.

She awoke late the following morning, and after a leisurely breakfast George, one of the tractor drivers, kept her talking, then Mrs Meeson's daughter arrived with her newly born infant. Finally she had to pay a visit to Mr Brooksby.

It was dark when she arrived at Mirbeck, the light from the farmhouse shining like a beacon over the moor. She had never been so glad to be home. Driving into the yard, Maggie switched off the engine and got out. Her father was already at the door awaiting her.

"Couldn't believe my ears when I heard your car," he said giving her a kiss on the cheek. "What happened? You weren't due back until Sunday."

"I phoned you last night but there was no reply."

Mr Kerr gave her a shrewd look. "Come in my girl. What you need is a good cup of tea."

If only tea would solve my problems thought Maggie as she sat sipping the hot strong liquid by the fire.

"I'm not engaged to Joel anymore."

Mr Kerr gave her a slow smile. "I never thought you would marry young Joel somehow — felt it in my bones."

"Oh Dad, everything's gone wrong in my life."

"Not everything. Your agent phoned. Will you ring back."

Maggie nodded. "Where's Polly? I didn't see her in the yard."

Mr Kerr's face took on a depressed look. "She got run over a few days ago. Wandered onto the Lazonby road. There's some mad drivers about. They couldn't care less. The vet said she was in such a bad way it was best to put her out of her misery." He paused and looked at Maggie.

"It won't be the same without Polly."

He nodded. "I was very fond of that dog. I'll miss her. I had taken the precaution of saving one of the puppies from her last litter. But it'll take a long time to train her. I'll have to be patient."

Maggie went up to her room. Despite the bad news about Polly it was good to be back. How faded the curtains were. She ought really to make a new pair. And as she went across to the window to close them, Venus was visible for a moment before disappearing behind a bank of clouds, and she remembered the first time she had viewed it through Drew's telescope.

She must stop thinking about Drew. She must make a concerted effort, block him from her mind and heart, and the best way to do that was to get a job as quickly as possible. Then she would be either too busy or too tired to think.

Maggie awoke the next morning in a resolute mood and immediately breakfast was over she phoned her agent.

"Hello Charles," she breezed gaily down the phone trying to pretend she hadn't a care in the world. "It's Maggie

243

here, Maggie Kerr. You phoned while I was away."

"Oh yes, Maggie," came Charles Pemworth's drawl. "Unfortunately the audition was yesterday. Liz Bradley got it. Weren't you with her at Lazonby. Nice girl. Just right. Of course if you had been there you would have got it like a shot. Keep in touch, although there's nothing coming up for a bit."

Maggie put the phone down with a heavy heart. She'd got to do something. Hotel work perhaps — just until another audition came up. She would ring her friend Greer. Greer knew everything that was happening.

The phone call was postponed because Mr Kerr wanted to go to Keswick cattle market to buy some ewes. "Come with me Maggie," he suggested. "Groceries are low and it's a good day out."

It was a good day. Mr Kerr was pleased with his purchase of sturdy Cheviot ewes. Maggie stocked up with groceries and met a couple of old friends. It was late when they returned, and as they entered the house the phone started ringing.

"Maggie!" said a familiar masculine voice.

Maggie felt a tingling down her spine. "Drew. Where are you?"

"Kingsley Magna as if you could care where I am. Got back last night. What did you mean rushing off like that without a word. You could at least have pushed a message under my door."

"I'm sorry about that."

"I should think you are. I was out of my mind with worry. I couldn't think what had happened."

"Couldn't you?" said Maggie coldly.

"I've had problems with Irina," Drew continued in a depressed voice.

Something snapped in Maggie. Listening to the details of the reconciliation was the last straw.

"Look Drew, I have to go. We'll continue this conversation some other time."

"But Maggie, hear me out . . . "

"I'm sorry."

She put the phone down, her hand was trembling.

"Give me a job to do Dad."

"You can take the milk out to the calves."

★ ★ ★

A week later Maggie's spirits were still low. She had phoned Greer who suggested her uncle's hotel at Wasdale. He was looking for help in the office, answering the phone, book-keeping, making out bills. "You could learn it in a day," Greer had said. Maggie had said she'd let him know.

There seemed to be no joy in life. Maggie put the vacuum cleaner away. She had done her usual morning chore of calf feeding and as she sat with a cup of coffee looking across the valley she thought of her phone call to her agent yesterday. He had told her there might be something in the New Year but he couldn't promise. Her career that had started off so well had reached an all-time low, and when she thought of Drew, which had become a daily habit, she felt nothing but defeat and humiliation.

Suddenly she knew what she had to do. She would climb a fell. She had always done it in the past when she was unhappy or uncertain what to do. The problem that existed in the valley vanished on the felltop.

She started to feel better as she changed into a pair of trousers, a thick sweater and kagool then looked for her climbing boots. She was the biggest fool on earth — falling in love with a married man. Well, she'd just have to fall out of love with him.

Then writing a quick note to her father — 'Have decided to climb Roman Fell. Don't worry will be back before dark. Love Maggie', she left it propped up by the telephone in the hall so he could see it the moment he returned, she set off on the short drive to the foot of the fell near the shores of Gawes Water.

The weather looked unsettled, there were dark clouds overhead, but she was not worried. She had done this climb before and was familiar with the area.

She parked the car at the far end of the lake. She seemed to be the only climber in the valley. Ahead of her loomed Roman Fell in the shape of the letter 'T'. She changed into her climbing boots and it was then she saw the slow puncture. By the time she returned from the felltop it would be dark and she had forgotten to bring a torch. There was nothing for it but to change the wheel now.

Not having the correct tools made the job take longer than it should and by the time she had washed her hands in the mountain stream that roared over the rocks nearby she had lost half an hour, and to make matters worse it started to rain.

She was not going back. She had made up her mind she was climbing

Roman Fell and she was not going home until she had done so. First she had to cross the mountain stream, finding stepping stones about twenty yards up, then the climb started.

At first the terrain was not too bad, climbing through knots of ferns, disturbing the occasional sheep who ran away with a mournful bleat. After about half an hour's climbing she sat down for a rest. The rain was light and did not trouble her, and as she looked down into the valley at the dark blue sheen of the lake and beyond to the Western Fells the pain in her heart started to ease. Here was peace, with the sheep, the birds, the soft grass and ferns. She felt she could stay there forever.

The rain eased off as she climbed a rocky staircase, a strong wind pulling at her hair. Pied wagtails swooped and all the time her spirits were rising. It was when she sat down for a rest in a grassy hollow she saw the mist coming up fast, blotting out the valley below. But there was no need to be alarmed, she was following a time-worn path along the top of the ridge. How could she get into any kind of trouble?

She continued on. The ridge now rising rapidly. Fifteen minutes later the mist came down. It was so sudden and complete — like walking into a dense fog. There was a swift drop in temperature and her hands stung with the cold. She was still on the path and so long as she kept to it there would be no problem.

On and on she climbed, slower now as the thick clammy mist swirled about her. She decided when she reached the Roman road that ran across the far end of the ridge she would turn back. It was years since she had seen the Roman road, must have been when she was a schoolgirl and went climbing with father on one of their infrequent visits to Cumbria. Was she trying to turn back the clock, recapture the blissful years of her early teens, before life became complicated.

Suddenly she splashed through a small pool of water and looked down. She had strayed from the path! How could she have been so foolish. The path was her lifeline. And suddenly like someone blind her sense of direction had gone. She stood still and peered through the mist. Directly ahead of her a dark shape loomed. Was it a rock? A cairn of stones? She walked quickly towards it. It was a cairn.

She sat down leaning her back against the stones. Cairns were not far from paths, but was it to the right or left? Drew had once told her if you're lost find a stream and follow it. Streams flow into rivers and rivers mean sooner or later human habitation. She listened hard for the sound of running water, but there was nothing, not even the sound of a bird. A few minutes ago she had been so confident.

She opened her knapsack and took out an apple. There was always the chance a wind would spring up and blow the mist away. When she had finished the apple, she ate the chocolate. The minutes seemed like hours, and she grew cold and stiff. She could die here and suddenly all the things she had ever worried about seemed trivial and unimportant.

She stood up, stamping her feet in the springy heather and blowing on her hands. The important thing was to keep warm. If there was a chance of dying from exposure waiting for the mist to rise, should she take a chance and plunge into the mist in the vain hope of finding the elusive path?

Suddenly she heard the sound of a boot striking a stone. It came again; then the yellow glow of a torch shone through the mist.

"Wait!" she called half running and stumbling as the yellow glow moved away from her direction. The yellow glow stopped.

"Maggie!" came a masculine voice, drifting, floating through the mist.

It was Drew's voice! She was dreaming. She must be. How could he possibly be on Roman Fell? Then suddenly she staggered into his arms not knowing whether to laugh or cry.

"Drew!" she gasped. "It is you. I thought I was dreaming."

His hand stroked her damp hair.

"Yes, my darling. It's me."

"But how did you know I was up here?" she asked bewilderedly.

"Messages by phones are meant to be read."

"I still don't understand. Why are you in Cumbria at all?"

"When a certain young woman puts the phone down on me I have no alternative."

He took her by the arm and together they stumbled over tufts of cotton grass, squelching through a boggy area. The mist started to thin out and then suddenly they walked into bright evening sunshine. Before them lay the old Roman road pitted by centuries of wind and rain winding its way across the flat plateau of the felltop. They sat down a short distance from the road and Drew brought out a flask of coffee pouring it into two plastic cups.

"You think of everything," said Maggie contentedly sipping the hot liquid.

"You should never go climbing alone."

Maggie looked crest-fallen. "I wanted to be alone to think."

"About what?"

"My career for a start. Things couldn't be worse. I've got a feeling I'm going to be out of work for a very long time. A friend has offered me a hotel job in Wasdale. I'm not sure what to do. Perhaps I should give up the theatre."

"Give up the theatre!" Drew exclaimed. "Didn't you tell me you'd like to have your own company. What's happened to that idea?"

"The same as all the other ideas — shelved, forgotten."

"Remember 'The Merchant of Venice'?" he asked. "An end of term play at Drama School and Joel

254

persuaded me to go along. Remember?"

Maggie remembered.

"The moon shines bright . . . " Drew began.

" . . . 'in such a night as this'," Maggie continued in a soft dreamy voice. "'When the sweet wind did gently kiss the trees, And they did make no noise, in such a night' . . . " Maggie's voice trailed off.

"Look Maggie, I've been thinking about your theatrical career. You've had four years experience in provincial rep. and I've seen you perform. You have beauty, intelligence, and stage presence, all you need is a chance. Now instead of sitting around waiting for some theatrical producer to come along, start your own theatrical company."

"I need capital. My meagre savings wouldn't last long. I did think of renting a hall in . . . "

"I've got a better idea," Drew cut in. "You can have the Long Gallery at Kingsley Magna — turn it into a theatre. It will be the only moated

255

theatre in England and you'll be near enough to Stratford to get the tourists. Must be well advertised . . . "

Maggie put her arms round Drew. "What a marvellous idea."

"I haven't finished yet," Drew smiled. "I'll finance you for six months. If you're not showing a profit by that time . . . "

"But I will show a profit. I'm certain of it. I have a number of ideas I'd like to discuss. For example why not give audiences . . . "

Drew suddenly kissed her on the mouth. "Don't you want to hear my ideas?"

"You can give me your ideas when we're back at Kingsley Magna." Drew gave her a soft look, as his arm tightened round her waist. "And I've spoken to your father. He wants to give the farm another year, but I think he'll be coming back."

"Thanks, Drew."

Then Maggie's eyes clouded as suddenly all her happiness evaporated.

"What's the matter, Maggie?" Drew asked softly.

"I'm such a fool," she whispered. "I had forgotten about Irina."

"What about Irina?" he asked giving her a slow smile.

"Stop being so infuriating Drew. You're married to her. You were reconciled in Leningrad."

"That is just where you're wrong. The divorce is going ahead."

"It's going ahead?" asked Maggie bewilderedly. "But Irina was weeping in that Chinese bar. And you looked so defeated I was certain, particularly when you didn't phone . . . "

"I can explain. I did try last week on the phone but you wouldn't give me a chance."

Maggie gave Drew a sheepish look. "I'm sorry, Drew. Have you had a hard time?"

He nodded. "Irina exceeded all expectations. A divorce was the last thing she wanted — I gathered her lover had gone back to his wife. Then she really hit below the belt. Threatened to go to Dad with the story that the whole thing was a pack of lies and the receipt a forgery. It was a conspiracy I had dreamed up to get rid of her." Drew gave a big sigh. "Dad always had a soft spot for Irina. He'd believe her. The night I saw you in the Chinese bar I was feeling desperate."

"You haven't explained why she disappeared from the tour company and where she went," queried Maggie.

"She disappeared in Moscow to put Ashley Morris in a hot seat for a while."

"But why?" asked Maggie amazed at this information.

"He wouldn't give her a better contract — more money, better billing, etc., etc. The arguing had been going on for years so she decided to bring matters to a head by disappearing."

"But where did she disappear to?" Maggie demanded.

"Golensk. She had a special visa for visiting relations, Nikolai was right."

"But not right about you going there without permission."

Drew gave a wry smile. "I'm afraid I've had second thoughts about Nikolai. He came to the hotel just before we left and I told him where to go."

"Did Irina get the better contract?"

Drew shook his head. "When Irina decided to disappear in Moscow and reappear in Leningrad she didn't make allowances for Ashley's temper. By the time he saw her his nerves were frayed and when Irina started her impossible demands — she wanted her salary doubled and she was already overpaid, the poor man snapped and fired her. Poor Irina. She was distraught. Her career means more than anything.

"It was after seeing that tragic look on your face in the Chinese bar I got the idea of a compromise. I told her if I got her job back would she agree to a divorce. She agreed. After we left the bar we went to Ashley's hotel and talked well into the night. That is why you didn't get your phone call, Maggie, my darling. It was so late when we had reached an agreement I took a room there for the night, only to discover when I got back to our hotel, you had gone."

"I'm sorry Drew, but I thought . . . "

"It's all in the past now."

Drew's arms went around her, drawing her close to him. Then he kissed her. It was a long kiss that radiated heat throughout her chilled body, bringing a flush to her cheeks, a shine to her eyes.

"Never leave me again," he muttered huskily. "I can't live without you. This last week has been sheer misery."

"It has for me too," she murmured.

"Will you marry me?" he asked gazing into Maggie's eyes humbly, beseechingly.

Her eyes gave him his answer. Then a small frown marred his face.

"There may be a bit of time to wait until the divorce is through."

"I'll wait forever," she replied simply, her voice choking with emotion.

The light was fading rapidly as they started their descent to the valley and in the south-west the moon appeared casting its flawless white light on the rugged Cumbrian fellside and to Maggie and Drew it held the same magic quality as on that unforgettable night.

THE END

WITH SOMEBODY ELSE
Theresa Charles

Rosamond sets off for Cornwall with Hugo to meet his family, blissfully unaware of the shocks in store for her.

A SUMMER FOR STRANGERS
Claire Hamilton

Because she had lost her job, her flat and she had no money, Tabitha agreed to pose as Adam's future wife although she believed the scheme to be deceitful and cruel.

VILLA OF SINGING WATER
Angela Petron

The disquieting incidents that occurred at the Vatican and the Colosseum did not trouble Jan at first, but then they became increasingly unpleasant and alarming.

DOCTOR NAPIER'S NURSE
Pauline Ash

When cousins Midge and Derry are entered as probationer nurses on the same day but at different hospitals they agree to exchange identities.

A GIRL LIKE JULIE
Louise Ellis

Caroline absolutely adored Hugh Barrington, but then Julie Crane came into their lives. Julie was the kind of girl who attracts men without even trying.

COUNTRY DOCTOR
Paula Lindsay

When Evan Richmond bought a practice in a remote country village he did not realise that a casual encounter would lead to the loss of his heart.

ENCORE
Helga Moray

Craig and Janet realise that their true happiness lies with each other, but it is only under traumatic circumstances that they can be reunited.

NICOLETTE
Ivy Preston

When Grant Alston came back into her life, Nicolette was faced with a dilemma. Should she follow the path of duty or the path of love?

THE GOLDEN PUMA
Margaret Way

Catherine's time was spent looking after her father's Queensland farm. But what life was there without David, who wasn't interested in her?

HOSPITAL BY THE LAKE
Anne Durham

Nurse Marguerite Ingleby was always ready to become personally involved with her patients, to the despair of Brian Field, the Senior Surgical Registrar, who loved her.

VALLEY OF CONFLICT
David Farrell

Isolated in a hostel in the French Alps, Ann Russell sees her fiancé being seduced by a young girl. Then comes the avalanche that imperils their lives.

NURSE'S CHOICE
Peggy Gaddis

A proposal of marriage from the incredibly handsome and wealthy Reagan was enough to upset any girl — and Brooke Martin was no exception.